THE ULTIMATE CURE

Ruth Richards came to Jersey expecting to work in a quiet old-fashioned practice. Instead she found a house like a minia- ture castle surrounded by all the trappings of wealth—and a household undermined by secret passions . . .

Having written fiction and non-fiction for children of all ages for many years, Jennifer Eden turned to writing Doctor Nurse Romances first as a challenge, then with increasing enjoyment as a new creative world opened up for her. She is very lucky in having a good back-up team of a husband and two sons with medical and dental qualifications. Having also experienced the other side of medicine as a patient, she hopes she is able to convey something of that with understanding too.

Jennifer Eden has written four other Doctor Nurse Romances, *Nurse on Approval*, *Stop-Gap Doctor*, *Surgeon in Retreat* and *A Surgeon's Hands*.

THE ULTIMATE CURE

BY

JENNIFER EDEN

MILLS & BOON LIMITED
ETON HOUSE   18–24 PARADISE ROAD
RICHMOND   SURREY TW9 ISR

*First published in Great Britain 1987
by Mills & Boon Limited*

© *Jennifer Eden 1987*

*Australian copyright 1987
Philippine copyright 1987*

ISBN 0 263 75781 1

*Set in Monotype Times 11 on 11 pt.
03-0787-55062*

*Typeset in Great Britain by
Associated Publishing Services
Printed and bound in Great Britain by
William Collins*

CHAPTER ONE

FROM 10,000 feet the sea looked like a sheet of crumpled green silk, inserted in places with bands of frothy white lace. Ruth woke from a short nap and looked drowsily at her watch. It was nearing the end of the one and a half hour flight from Norwich, and they should be landing in Jersey at any minute now.

As the small plane began its descent the group of Channel Islands became recognisable, individual shapes, and Ruth easily picked out Sark and Alderney, Guernsey and, lastly, her destination, Jersey. This was her first visit to the Isles but she had been reading up on them ever since receiving Sarah's phone call.

Ruth still felt bemused at the speed with which events had overtaken her since that day. After weeks of inaction she had suddenly been caught up in what had seemed a maelstrom of violent upheaval, giving her no chance for second thoughts. It was too late now, she told herself, to start having regrets—but one regret would persist. It was that she was about to start a job as a nurse-receptionist in general practice instead of in her old hospital as a staff nurse. Still, it was only a temporary set-back—there would be another vacancy for a staff nurse later in the autumn, and she hoped to be back in her old teaching hospital long before then.

The debilitating effects of anaemia that had almost snatched the triumph of passing her finals out of her grasp, had also been the reason why she had lost the coveted post of staff nurse. The joy of getting her nursing qualifications after three years of work and study had turned into deep disappointment at being told she wasn't yet fit enough to take on a job of responsibility. That it would be best if she went home to recuperate and not think of returning to hospital work until her own doctor passed her as fit.

The Senior Nursing Tutor at St Catherine's had taken it as a personal affront that one of her most promising students had allowed herself to become anaemic in the first place. She put it all down to Ruth's habit of eating snacks at odd moments rather than sitting down to a proper meal—that, in her opinion, accounted for the lack of iron in Ruth's system!

But Ruth wasn't entirely to blame for her low red cell count. When excessive tiredness, breathlessness and mild palpitations finally forced her to seek medical advice and the abnormality of her haemoglobin was diagnosed, it was also discovered that there was a lack of certain chemicals in her body essential for the absorption of iron. She was put on an iron-rich and protein-rich diet supplemented by a course of liver injections—then packed off home to Norfolk to be nursed back to full health by her mother.

Ruth felt as if she had been sent home in disgrace. 'Nonsense,' said her mother, looking forward to the chance to practise her old skills. 'That's just depression talking—and after three months of this wretched illness, who wouldn't be depressed.'

To Ruth, the weeks of her mother's careful nursing passed in a vacuum of inertia. She tried not to show how much she missed the crucial activity of the hospital round—the company of friends her own age and the mateyness of the nurses' home. Her habitual smile was hard to come by during those days of convalescence, and her round dimpled cheeks markedly lacked colour. Her mother became so concerned about her that Sarah's sudden phone call had come as a deliverance to them both.

Sarah Froy had trained with Ruth, but had qualified six months earlier. She was now an agency nurse, preferring short spells of temporary work to a full-time job as this gave her more freedom to be with her baby son. She was not married and still lived at home with her parents. A temporary job as nurse/receptionist in Jersey had already been arranged for her when another job in her own home town had become available, and as far as Sarah was concerned that was it! The agency promised to release her from the Jersey contract providing she could find another qualified nurse to take her place at such short notice.

'You *will* take over for me in Jersey, won't you Ruth?' she had begged desperately over the phone. 'It's only for a month—until the permanent nurse recovers from her operation. They won't mind who turns up as long as somebody does, and I'll send on all your particulars. Yes, it's in general practice—a Dr Matthew Owens, The Surgery, St Swithin. Got that? Any time you want me to do you a favour in return . . . Yes, I know I can't conjure up a post as staff nurse for you—but think of the nice, warm glow of self-satisfaction you'll experience knowing how happy you have made a certain adorable little poppet, to say nothing of his loving mother!'

Ruth had replaced the phone feeling that what she was experiencing was not a warm glow of self-satisfaction so much as panic at being drawn into a situation fraught with doubt and misgivings. She didn't know the first thing about being a nurse/

receptionist in general practice.

Her mother had brushed her fears aside. 'You'll soon pick it up, it will come easy after the hospital, and a month in Jersey is just what you need right now.' Mrs Richards' clear blue eyes had lost something of their fretted look and she radiated a mixture of relief and pleasure. 'The whole of September by the sea—what a wonderful rest cure.'

'Mother, anyone listening to you would think I was going there to enjoy myself. I'm going there to work, remember!'

It had always amazed Carole Richards that a daughter of hers appeared so uninterested in the opposite sex. Ruth liked the company of men but only on a take-them-or-leave-them kind of basis; there had been no emotional involvement with any of the male companions she brought home from time to time. When tackled about it, which was often, for Carole hoped to be a grandmother before she was fifty, Ruth had answered off-handedly that she 'hadn't got the time for that sort of thing'. But Carole suspected that she was that rarity for these days—an old-fashioned romantic waiting for Mr Right to come along. Her father had been like that, there had only ever been one woman in his life, and Carole had been that lucky woman.

Ruth was like her father in other ways too, in looks and disposition and in a warm-hearted, impulsive nature. He had died the year Ruth left school to start her training as a nurse, and his loss had stamped Carole's face with the first lines of suffering she had ever known, lines that deepened when she smiled, as she did now. 'There's no law against mixing both,' she said pointedly.

Now looking down from the plane, Ruth could see that the tiny blue lozenges she had been trying to identify for the past few seconds were looming nearer and revealing themselves as swimming-pools in the grounds of the many hotels. The island was a checker-board of tiny multi-coloured fields bordered with golden beaches and crystal seas, and with an overall greenness like a reposing backdrop against the patches of bright flowering gardens. The airport was busier and grander than she had expected for such a small island, and the Norwich plane when it landed was dwarfed by neighbouring jets.

Sarah had instructed her to stand by the bookstall and wait until someone came along to claim her. 'I've sent on your particulars and given Dr Owens a detailed description of you,' she had assured Ruth when she phoned again.

'And what about a detailed description of Dr Owens for me?'

'Oh lord, don't say you haven't received my letter? It had the photograph the agency sent me of Dr Owens enclosed in it, and I posted it first class too! Well, in case you don't get it in time, I'll tell you what he looks like—about sixty, tall, white-haired. I'm afraid that's all I can remember.'

'Thanks, that's a great help. I should think that description would fit about fifty per cent of the men travelling to Jersey in any one day. I only hope your letter gets to me in time.'

But of course it didn't, and Ruth wondered whether Sarah had forgotten to post it or had even addressed it wrongly—she wouldn't put it past her. Sarah had a streak of irresponsibility in her that was at direct variance with her otherwise down-to-earth nature.

So Ruth took up her position at the bookstall and waited—and waited—and waited. She stared so fixedly at every white-haired man who came

anywhere near that she earned herself some very
odd looks in return. Perhaps Sarah had even got the
time wrong. Ruth could see the cafeteria quite near
and longed to go across and get herself a cup of tea
but was frightened to leave her post, thinking it
would be just her luck for Dr Owens to come along
as soon as she was missing.

Suddenly she became aware that she was being
watched by a man leaning nonchalantly against a
counter on the opposite wall. He was tall, but that
was the only thing he had in common with the
errant Dr Owens. His hair was dark, not white, and
he looked about thirty-five—but the colour of his
hair and his eyes and his age were immaterial to the
forceful impact he suddenly had on Ruth.

She had inherited more than looks and disposition
from her father, she had also inherited his lively
imagination—an imagination that had made a liveli-
hood out of writing popular westerns when he had
never stepped foot outside his own country, an
imagination that sometimes went into overdrive as
Ruth's did now.

This stranger opposite involuntarily materialised
as the embodiment of all she had ever looked for in
the man of her dreams. It was not an expression she
used to herself, she only knew that some time,
somewhere, she would suddenly encounter a man of
whom she could say 'this is the one I have been
waiting for.' And there he stood, looking at her with
brooding shadowy eyes as if he too had seen in her
someone he felt he had known from a previous age.

As a matter of fact Matt Owens was wondering
to himself who the devil she could be. He had
watched her, struggling along with her case on
wheels, ever since she had claimed it from the
baggage chute and made her way with difficulty to

the bookstall. There, the case had fallen on to its side for about the third time and she had seemed to give up and had stayed where she was, looking about her in a lost bewildered kind of way.

Matt's practised eye could tell she had only recently recovered from a long illness, there was a translucent sheen to her skin that told its own story. Her unnatural pallor emphasised the brilliance of her widely spaced blue eyes. They looked enormous beneath a fringe of thick golden hair, and when she turned her head to stare anxiously towards the exit he could see that her hair continued down her back as far as her waist. A slender waist, too slender to sustain plumpness—not that she was plump by any means, but she possessed curves where curves were most appreciated.

Matt found his curiosity aroused. Many girls came from the mainland for seasonal work in Jersey, mostly as waitresses and chambermaids in the hotels—but it was a bit late in the year for seasonal work now. If she had been taller and slimmer with shorter hair he might have thought she was the girl he was getting a bit fed up with waiting for, but the description didn't tally. It seemed a bit odd though, that they should both be standing here waiting for somebody. He decided to go over and speak to her.

Seeing him approaching Ruth suddenly felt her heart pounding against her ribs, bringing with it a feeling of suffocation. It was one thing to nurse the image of a dream hero ever since she had reached the age of puberty, but it was quite another thing to come face to face with such a dream in reality. He might not measure up to the man she had conjured out of her imagination and then her dream bubble would burst. But as he drew nearer she realised her imagination for once had fallen far short of the real thing.

This man was flesh and bone; there was real fire in his eyes, there was strength in the line of his jaw and a mobility about the set of his mouth. His hair was not wholly dark; where light caught it it shone like bronze, and his eyes were hazel not black, but there was something else too that touched her like a vibration, and that was his air of haunting sadness. It gave a severity to his expression that Ruth found daunting, and when he scowled as he did now, he looked formidable. Matt wasn't aware he was scowling—frowning yes, which was a habit of his when puzzled, and this fair girl's obvious agitation was puzzling him.

His approach was very direct. 'Are you feeling all right?' he asked, and for Ruth, his abrupt clipped way of speaking was another damper to her dreams. To live up to his image he should have spoken in a deep caressing, velvety voice.

'I'm perfectly all right, thank you,' she answered stiffly, turning away so that he shouldn't see the tell-tale rise of colour to her cheeks.

Matt studied her profile and seeing that her full bottom lip was trembling very slightly, felt a sudden compunction for her. She looked so young and vulnerable—she reminded him of a child travelling on her own for the first time, full of fears and doubts of the unknown. She was obviously dressed for the occasion in a very new and becoming outfit of turquoise blue trousers with matching jacket which gave her a false air of sophistication. He wondered if this child had ever been out of her mothers's sight before.

'You don't look all right,' he persisted. 'You look very worried. Are you worried? You don't have to be, you know. There is always someone at airports to advise unaccompanied girls. What is this—your first trip away from home?'

Ruth tried to freeze him with a look, but that was impossible with large soulful eyes like hers. 'For your information,' she said, tilting her chin proudly, 'I happen to be a fully-qualified nurse and I've come to Jersey to do a very important job.'

He stared at her incredulously—he had taken her for a sixteen-year-old fresh from school, and he felt affronted that she had put him in the wrong. 'You'll be telling me next that your name is Sarah Froy,' he said laconically.

Ruth gaped. 'Sarah! Do you know Sarah?'

'I'm not on first-name terms with her as you seem to be.' His eyes glittered with a grim humour as an idea suddenly occurred to him. 'I was supposed to be meeting her here, but she hasn't turned up—and *you* seem to be acquainted with her. More than a coincidence, don't you think? My name is Matthew Owens; does that mean anything to you?'

Ruth wailed inwardly, 'Oh Sarah, what have you done to me?' A sensation of fluttering rose in her throat which she tried to swallow back, but couldn't because her mouth was too dry. 'I—I'm Ruth Richards,' she said nervously. 'And I'm afraid there's been some mistake. I—I've come in place of my friend Sarah. She promised to write to you and explain, but something must have prevented her. And—and you're not a bit like the description she gave me of you—' Ruth's voice rose on a note of accusation, she felt that somehow she had been tricked. She wished she had never embarked on this wild-goose chase, both Sarah and her mother had persuaded her against her better judgement. In her wretchedness Ruth was ready to blame everybody but herself.

'There does seem to be some almighty mix-up,' came Matthew Owens' impatient rejoinder, 'but we'd better sort that out when we get back to the surgery. How do I know you are who you say you are?'

'And how do I know you are Dr Matthew Owens?' Ruth answered with spirit, losing her apologetic air. She was rapidly coming out of the spell of her dream world and facing up to reality. 'I have papers from the nursing agency to prove who I am, but why should I believe you are Dr Owens? Sarah said he had white hair and was about sixty.'

'Sarah, bless her sweet muddled little hide, was describing my father—also Dr Matthew Owens. My friends call me Matt to distinguish us. If you still doubt me ask the lady over there, she's one of our patients—' and he pointed to a silver-haired, late middle-aged woman seated near the cafeteria who had been watching them both with some interest.

'I believe you,' said Ruth, suppressing a sigh of resignation. Silently she watched as Matt picked up her case, and silently she followed him out of the airport to a waiting car.

It was nearly an hour later before Ruth got her much needed cup of tea, and that was in a small back room at St Swithin House.

She couldn't recall much of the drive from the airport. She was conscious of narrow twisting roads congested with traffic, and great banks of brilliant blue hydrangeas at the wayside and in gardens, and climbing up the walls of stone cottages. There was something blue everywhere she looked—blue skies and blue seas and the blue flowers.

Matt Owens was a skilful driver, edging his sleek foreign car along the tortuous bends with ease, his long slender fingers relaxed on the steering-wheel.

He was a fit-looking man without an ounce of superfluous flesh on his bones, a man who drove himself hard Ruth suspected—and also those who worked for him? It was a chilling thought.

The road to St Swithin climbed steadily upwards, for once straight though still narrow, little more than a bridle path in places and finally plunging into a tunnel of trees that entwined their branches low overhead. Here the sun had a faint translucent light as if strained through a green sieve. There was no sound, the close set leaves deadened all noise, then when they approached the end of the tunnel they burst out into startling brightness and the twilight world of silence and filtered light erupted into a dazzling spectacle of green cliffs, heather-covered headlands, glistening rocks and the wide engulfing sea.

Ruth gasped with surprise and delight and for the first time since leaving the airport her companion smiled. 'It's a spectacular view, isn't it,' he said. 'I always bring first-time visitors this way, along Back Lane, just to watch their reactions.'

He was well-rewarded with Ruth's reaction. Tears of joy sprang to her eyes, tears not entirely due to the loveliness her surroundings. She was still emotionally high, still affected by all that had happened to her in recent weeks, and then the unfortunate misunderstanding at the airport hadn't helped.

'Is this St Swithin?' she asked tremulously.

'Part of it—the best part to my mind. You'll find St Swithin a long-drawn-out narrow town. It wasn't planned, it just grew.' At a junction he turned the car on to a metalled road and the noise and roar of traffic swallowed them up once more. The town was a mixed community of large houses, small farms and tiny cottages. There were fashionable shops and a large modern school, but also a more historic quarter where names over the shop windows had their roots in the Norman Conquest. And joining the old and the new was a network of tiny meadows that looked such a novelty to Ruth after the vast barley prairies of rural Norfolk.

They turned off the road into a short lane and then through stone walls into the grounds of a large house. Ruth took it to be a hotel until Dr Owens said: 'Well, here we are. Let's see if we can now sort out this mess.' Ruth stared up at the house, overawed by its grandeur. It reminded her of an old French château with its round turrets and squat arches and thick ivy-clad granite walls, a reddish coloured granite that glowed in the sun.

'It's beautiful—it's beautiful,' she exclaimed involuntarily. 'It looks like something out of a fairy story. It can't be a *surgery*!' She looked up at the man beside her with wide disbelieving eyes.

He nodded, faintly amused. 'Just a part of it—the rest is my father's home.' He raised his eyebrows questioningly. 'Like you, I am just a bird of passage, come to help out when needed.'

He lifted her case without effort then led her through one of the archways to a cobbled courtyard. Beyond, Ruth could see the ground falling away amid pine trees to the sea, and could hear the distant surge and pull of waves against rocks and cliffs. They went on through a door into a cavernous kitchen, where a girl of about eighteen, chopping vegetables at a wooden table, looked up startled at their sudden appearance.

Dr Owens nodded to her. 'Anybody around, Pam?'

'Dr Raynor is out on calls and Mrs Miller has taken Robbie to St Helier on the three o'clock bus.'

The girl spoke with a slight Lancashire accent.

Robbie, Dr Raynor, Mrs Miller, said Ruth to herself, memorising the names for future reference, little knowing at this moment how inextricably the lives of these three unknowns would be caught up with hers in the weeks to come.

'Any phone calls for me?' Dr Owens asked.

'Yes, from England—from a Miss Froy. She wants you to ring back. I took her number.'

'Pamela always refers to the mainland as England, I think she looks upon Jersey as a foreign country,' the doctor remarked dryly as he led Ruth along a shadowy passage-way between thick walls. 'Perhaps now we'll get to the bottom of this mix-up, so if you wait here I'll go and see what it's all about.'

The room he ushered Ruth into struck her as cold and little used. It was dominated by a large rounded wall at the far end with narrow high windows which gave a limited view of the pine trees and sea beyond. With a slight feeling of unreality Ruth perched on the upholstered window-seat and took stock of her surroundings. In spite of the sun that filtered through the tall windows the light was dimmed by the effect of the heavy oak-panelled walls and solid dark furniture. It was an oppressive room, there were no flowers, no dainty touches to relieve the gloom, but there was an abundance of books lining two complete walls. Ruth wondered if in the past it had been a library or the smoking-room. Family photographs crowded the long mantelpiece, but they were portraits of a bygone age in heavy gilt frames taken even before the older Dr Owens' time, judging by the fashions. Though she was curious, Ruth lacked the confidence to go across and look at them. She was nervous—poised on the edge of the seat as if ready for flight any minute.

She heard footsteps approaching along the stone paved passage-way—a firm unhurried tread that seemed just right for Matt's lean muscular body. Already she was thinking of him as Matt and though in her present state of uncertainty she fervently wished she had never embarked on this mad enterprise, the image of his handsome melancholy face gave her a feeling of dangerous pleasure, and she knew that if she were given the choice she would stay just for the sake of seeing more of him.

The door opened and he came in, closing it behind him and leaning against it. He was smiling, which was a relief, yet as she had noticed before, his smiles were detached from any real warmth. They were just exercises in being polite. He had a habit too of raising his eyebrows at times which gave him a satanic look.

'The matter has now been cleared up,' he said in a manner that showed his exasperation. 'And all I can say about your colleague Sarah Froy is that it's a good thing for this practice she sent you in her place. A right mess she would have made of things, let loose here!'

'She's a jolly good nurse,' Ruth answered heatedly. Criticism of Sarah was in a way criticism of the hospital where they had both trained, and she wasn't going to have that. 'She may be a bit disorganised in her private life, but nobody could fault her professionally—'

'Disorganised!' Matt broke in with a hollow laugh. 'That's putting it mildly. Chaotic would be a better description. Can you guess what happened? No, you'll never guess, I'll tell you. Miss Froy has only just discovered that the letters to you and to my father are still in her handbag—in a special pocket where she keeps things so that she won't forget

them, she told me. She could swear blind—and that's
her own expression—that she had posted both letters.
She only discovered them an hour ago when she was
putting away another letter she didn't want to forget.
Now what can you say in her defence?'

It was a rhetorical question, he didn't expect an
answer. He went to the nearest chair and lowered
himself into it, stretching out his long legs and
clasping his hands behind his head. He had an
uncanny way of staring without blinking.

Ruth couldn't help herself, she dissolved into
laughter. She could just imagine Sarah's breathless
horrified explanations over the phone. Sarah had
been the despair of her tutors at times, yet she had
passed every exam with flying colours. When Ruth
laughed her dimples came into play—in her cheeks
and at the side of her mouth and one secretive little
one in her chin. The man frowned, wondering all at
once if it would be wise to introduce this provoca-
tively pretty little thing into a household that was
already undermined by hidden passions. Ruth looked
so vulnerable with her wide innocent eyes and child-
like expression, that he felt he wouldn't like to see
her hurt, which she could be if she became too
involved in their lives. Still, it was only for a month
and he felt reluctant to let her go because she
interested him, and outside his work and the one
love of his life there wasn't much to interest him
these days.

Tea was served, and while they were drinking
Matt explained the arrangements that had already
been made with the agency. For the first time Ruth
learnt that she wouldn't meet the older Dr Owens,
he had left the day before on a month's cruise. He
had been hoping to see the replacement nurse settled
in before going on holiday but the sailing time had

been put forward twenty-four hours, and everything had been rather hectic at the last minute. He had been particularly worried that he would not be able to keep his appointment at the airport.

'I put his mind at rest on that score,' Matt went on. 'I had already made arrangements to take a month's leave to cover him anyway. Dad needed that holiday, I wasn't going to let him postpone it. A Dr Raynor works part-time here as well. This is a busy practice and one doctor can't carry the load alone. When Mrs Sudbury, the regular nurse, found she was due to go into hospital for her hysterectomy this month, I promised I'd contact an agency in London for a temporary nurse to replace her. I'm domiciled in London by the way, at the University —working at St Jude's,' he explained in answer to Ruth's questioning look.

Ruth was impressed. St Jude's was one of the smaller colleges of the London University, and renowned for its scientific research. Many a well-known scientist had started on the path to eminence via its lecture halls and laboratories. Matt went on to explain further. His particular field of study was micro-biology, but he had had a grounding in his father's practice for some years prior to settling in London, and returned to Jersey whenever he could—'Just to keep my hand in,' he added, with one of his mirthless smiles. 'Anyway, the job's yours—that is if you think you can cope. Personally, I don't think you look all that well.'

This was the moment Ruth had dreaded, having to confess about her illness, thinking it would be another disadvantage against her, but the man opposite was perverse enough to shrug such doubts aside. 'A lot of girls your age get anaemia and learn to live with it. As long as you rest whenever you can and eat plenty of the right food, I don't see that it should make any difference. You won't find the work here all that arduous—nothing to compare with a London hospital. As a matter of fact you should be able to find time to laze around and build up your energy again. Mrs Miller, the house-keeper—' but whatever he had been going to say about Mrs Miller was cut short by the banging of an outer door. Matt raised his eyebrows. 'I think you are about to be introduced to some more members of the household,' he said laconically, and Ruth heard the sound of light footsteps running along the passage.

A small boy came into the room flushed from hurrying. He looked as if about to run towards the chair where Matt was sitting, but becoming aware of Ruth's presence he stopped short and stared warily at her with watchful golden-brown eyes. He was about six or seven, thin and tall—like his father? Ruth asked herself, and her heart fluttered with unexpected disappointment. The likeness between the man and boy was remarkable, but more notable still was the similar air of melancholy that marked their faces with a sense of unhappiness.

CHAPTER TWO

RUTH woke with a start, rolled on to her back, and stared around at her unfamiliar surroundings. At first she thought she was back in the troubled distorted dream from which she had just escaped into wakefulness, then realisation came flooding back—it hadn't been a dream; she was *here* in Jersey, and sleeping in the main guest room at St Swithin House!

She remembered now her mixed feelings of misgiving and awe when first shown the room where she was to sleep. It wasn't only its size and its lavish furnishings, including the four-poster bed—it was too grand and impersonal to be anybody's bedroom, it belonged by rights to a museum. She tried to show a gratitude she was far from feeling, knowing that she had Mrs Miller to thank for this well-meant gesture. Ruth had taken an instant liking to the housekeeper. She was a motherly, homely-looking person, reminding Ruth of Aunt Mildred, her father's sister, though Aunt Mildred had warm brown eyes whereas Mrs Miller's were pale-coloured and protuberant, their expression blurred by the thick glasses she wore. But even pebble glasses couldn't hide the light of triumph in them when she had announced after the evening meal: 'I'll show you up to your room now, Miss Richards. You are to sleep in what is known as the Prince's Room.'

The two left at the table, Matt and Dr Raynor, had not said anything at this, but Ruth got the impression from the glances they exchanged that the allocation of such a room to her had not met with their approval.

Dr Raynor had been another shock to her. When Matt had introduced Ruth to the tall woman with the beautifully groomed blonde hair and the alert appraising eyes, saying, 'This is Stephanie Raynor, my father's junior partner,' Ruth had heard herself stammering out some banal greeting in reply, and from then on had been struck dumb, only too conscious of her travel-stained clothes compared to the other's immaculate appearance. Dr Raynor's height and air of sophistication had put Ruth at a disadvantage too, and yet Stephanie had been more than friendly and had done her best to put the younger girl at ease.

Ruth groaned inwardly now as she slipped out of the high bed, and felt around for her slippers with her bare feet. She must have made an awful lot of gaffes the previous evening, becoming more and more unsure of herself as it had dawned on her that she had been pitchforked into a world different from anything she had known before. She had expected an easy little job in a quiet old-fashioned practice, instead of which here she was in a house like a miniature castle surrounded by all the trappings of wealth. Why ever did Dr Owens have to practise medicine when he owned all this? she asked herself.

She padded across to the turret which had been converted into a bathroom. In winter it must feel like an ice-box, even now at high summer it struck cold. It worried Ruth that there were no curtains at the narrow slit-like windows, though it didn't matter—she was only overlooked by pine trees. This room, like the study on the ground floor, was at the back of the house, giving magnificent views of the sea from the main windows.

Ruth had asked Mrs Miller why it was called the Prince's Room and the housekeeper had wrinkled her snub nose and looked coy. 'A certain prince was supposed to have slept here when he came to visit Jersey—some say to see Lily Langtry, the one they call the Jersey Lily. That was when it was called St Swithin Manor and belonged to the DeBrice family. Dr Matt's great-grandmother was a DeBrice and she married a Welshman—Thomas Owens.' Mrs Miller related the story with a familiarity due to repeated telling.

'You have been with the family a long time?' Ruth queried.

The older woman folded her arms across her ample bosom. 'It seems like it at times,' she answered cryptically. 'Actually I came here in the first place to look after Robbie; I used to be a nanny. That was three years ago when his mother—' She stopped short, and the eyes behind the thick glasses became cautious. 'Well, I won't keep you talking now, my dear,' she said, edging towards the door. 'You'll want to unpack and get to bed. Breakfast is at eight o'clock—the surgery opens at nine.'

When Robbie's mother what? Ruth had asked herself as she undressed. She had wondered about the missing Mrs Owens all evening, and had supposed at first that she had gone on the cruise with her father-in-law. Now Ruth surmised she had died. That seemed more feasible and would account for the sadness that seemed to haunt every expression that passed between father and child.

But there was something else too that could be the cause of the sadness and that was the fact that little Robbie couldn't speak. Ruth had at first put his silence down to shyness but as the afternoon grew into evening and he still hadn't uttered a word, she realised he had a disability. She could understand nothing being said about it in front of him, for he could hear well enough, but after he had gone to bed she had expected Matt to mention the matter to her and when he didn't she began to feel uncomfortable. Surely he wasn't ashamed of his son—or worse still one of those people who thought that if they could sweep a problem under the carpet nobody would know about it? Ruth wasn't like that herself and didn't understand it in others, so when an opportunity presented itself she brought up the subject of Robbie's muteness.

At the time, Matt was showing her over the wing of the house that they called The Surgery. It had its own entrance and waiting-room, treatment-room and pharmacy and two spare rooms fitted out as wards, used, Matt explained, for maternity patients who wanted to pay for that little bit of extra attention.

'Don't be alarmed,' he added dryly, correctly interpreting the look on Ruth's face. 'Babies come few and far between, so sometimes we take in the elderly instead who just want a rest—or perhaps their families want a rest from them. You won't be overworked and Mrs Miller will always help out. She used to be a nurse, though she's unqualified.'

'She must be invaluable,' Ruth answered admiringly.

Matt gave her a quick glance. 'Very!' he said, and his tone of voice left Ruth wondering.

She felt more at home in Nurse Sudbury's own little room, here she was in familiar territory. Everything had been left ready for her and drawers and cupboards marked so that she would know where things were kept. The equipment was all modern,

and she noted with some surprise that there was an
electronic sphygmomanometer. Matt saw her looking
at it and said: 'You haven't come across one of
these before? You'll find it quite easy to use, much
better than the old-style hand pumping instrument
for taking blood pressures. Here, sit down and I'll
demonstrate.'

She rolled up her sleeve and he wound the arm
cuff swiftly around her upper arm, and switched on.
Ruth felt the cuff tighten automatically, then came
a sharp metallic clattering as the print-out appeared.
It had taken less than a few seconds; she was
impressed and said so.

Matt tore off the print-out and read the result
aloud. 'One hundred and twenty-five over seventy-
five, nothing to give concern there—normal for your
age. I wouldn't bet on your blood count being
normal though. When did you last have a blood
test?' His hazel eyes brooded on her.

'When I was discharged from hospital. My red
cell count was normal then.'

'Hmm, I'd like to check that for myself—I'll run
you over to the hospital one day, and while we're
on that subject I'll just go over a few points about
the Jersey Health Scheme. D'you know anything
about it?' Ruth shook her head, and Matt rummaged
through a drawer in the desk and produced a booklet.
'Here's some bedtime reading to familiarise you,
you'll find it quite simple to remember. The scheme
differs from the National Health Service in some
respects. Hospital treatment is free, but GPs charge
fees commensurate with their services, then the
patient may recover through the scheme a fixed
amount which is called medical benefit. Any patient
who wishes to see a consultant privately must pay
his fees in full, but of course consultants may be

seen on referral at the Outpatients Clinic at the hospital free of charge. I think that covers the basic issues—you'll find everything else you need to know in that little booklet.' Matt eased himself out of the chair. 'Anything else you want to ask me while we're here?'

For Ruth that was an open invitation to ask the question that was burning in the back of her mind.

'I—I, well I—' she swallowed ineffectively, the words seemed to stick in her throat. If only he wouldn't stare in that unblinking way. 'It's—it's about Robbie. I—I thought at first that he was dumb, but as he can hear perfectly well, I just wondered—' her words trailed away as she watched all expression leave Matt's face, only the eyes remained alive and they darkened menacingly.

'No, you're right, he is not dumb,' he answered coldly. 'He just doesn't speak.'

'You mean he *could* speak if he wanted to!'

'I didn't say that.' Ruth realised by his tone of voice that she was pursuing a forbidden subject, but she couldn't give up.

'You mean his speechlessness was brought on by some traumatic shock—something like that?' her voice deepened the more agitated she became.

Matt strode across to the window, and stood with his back to her, a tall rigid figure, intimidating in his silence. She didn't expect him to answer, then he turned, silhouetted against the light, his face in shadow. 'Miss Richards, this is a painful subject and after this I never want to refer to it again. Three years ago my son suffered a severe shock and since then except for the occasional bout of coughing he hasn't uttered a sound. He was examined by an ear, nose and throat specialist at the time who found nothing physically wrong with him, and he was then referred to a psychiatrist who diagnosed hysterical aphonia—that, as you so naïvely described it, is speechlessness brought on by shock. Robbie has learnt to live with his disability, even to keep up with his school-work, but if any mention is made of it or of the *reason* for it, he becomes extremely distressed. That is why the subject is now taboo. I think my son will start to speak again in time, and I can afford to wait. Now, shall we rejoin Dr Raynor?'

Ruth felt that not only was the subject dismissed but that she was dismissed also. She was not sorry to escape from the forbidding figure whose very voice seemed a reproach. How could she mention the reason for Robbie's aphonia if she didn't even know it herself? And surely something could be done for the poor child—just to accept it was, to her, insufferable. It was no use telling herself that she would only be here, in Jersey, for four weeks—that she would walk out of their lives and never see any of these people again—she knew differently. Both Matt and the wistful small boy had made such an impression on her that even if she were never to see them again after her month was up, she could never forget them.

There was no shower in the turret, and the old-fashioned iron bath was so huge that Ruth felt she could have lost herself in it. She was quickly in and out and then into a leisure-suit of russet-coloured velour, her favourite wear for free time, and she had an hour and a half of free time before breakfast.

Her main desire at present was to get away from the nineteenth-century opulence of the Prince's Room. She found it oppressive and overwhelming and she made up her mind to ask Mrs Miller, when she knew her a bit better, if it was possible to move to another room.

She crept through the sleeping house down to the kitchen, and out into the courtyard, and found that the out-of-doors, unlike indoors, was awake and vibrant with sound. Magpies chattered aggressively at her from the pine trees, the roar of the sea rose above the sound of the wind rustling the dry fronds of the stunted palms, and a robin in a maple tree was rehearsing his autumn song. Ruth felt a sense of exhilaration sweep over her at the feel of the invigorating wind that was blowing directly from the sea. She began to run, releasing the pent-up nervous energy that had kept her on edge all the previous day, glorying in the exercise that she had been too tired to enjoy for weeks, telling herself that she was feeling much better—that Jersey was working its magic on her already.

She ran lightly across the lawn, down a flight of stone steps into a wilderness garden and on through more pine trees until she burst out breathlessly into the open near the cliffs.

There was no demarcation line between the grounds of St Swithin House and the wide cliff-top plateau of moss and cropped grass and low-growing scrub other than a public footpath that meandered along some yards inland from the cliff edge. It followed a winding course downwards until it met a narrow beach about half a mile further west. Ruth crossed it and stood on the pinnacle of the cliff top, feeling the wind tugging at her hair, and flattening her trousers against her legs. The sea spread out below her like a great turbulent blue bowl with fleeting cloud shadows passing over its ruffled waters. It was beautiful and sinister at the same time, merciless in its strength as it sent wave after wave crashing against the rocks at the base of the cliff.

Ruth didn't have a good head for heights, but she couldn't resist going a few inches closer to the edge so that she could look downwards. It was a sheer drop with part of the cliff jutting out like an upturned cave. She could see the shiny black forbidding interior, and the thought of losing her step and crashing down to certain death in that black pit made her shudder. Hastily she drew back, just as a voice nearby said laughingly: 'There now, you have spoilt the illusion, I thought you were some visiting sea-nymph poised for flight.'

Ruth swung round startled, surprised not so much by the unexpected voice as by the fact that she had neither seen nor heard anyone approaching.

A tall, bronzed man stood just a few feet off, grinning audaciously at her. His hair was fair, tightly curled and cropped short, and his grey eyes twinkled humorously. Perspiration hung in beads to his forehead and by the way he was dressed it didn't take any great powers of detection to see he was out jogging. That was why she hadn't noticed him, thought Ruth, he must have come up very swiftly while she was making her cautious way to the cliff edge.

'I can assure you I'm no nymph,' she retorted flippantly. 'I'm a very solid eight stone. I'm also——'

'No, don't tell me,' he stopped her, his grin widening. 'I like to kid myself that I can place any given person in their background. I go by their aura—your aura tells me you are in show business. I'd say the new musical opening in St Helier next week. A dancer? The soubrette?'

Just for a moment Ruth was tempted to play along with him, then realised there was the possibility that he lived locally and might even be a patient or a friend of the Owens, and Matt wouldn't take lightly to her playing such games. She assumed a mock contrite expression. 'Sorry to make a dent in your powers of clairvoyance, but I am not in show business, though sometimes it seems like it. I'm actually a nurse—temporarily—with Dr Owens.'

The man's expression visibly underwent a change, his smile vanished and a guarded, not to say slightly alarmed look, flickered in and out of his eyes.

'I see. Come to take the place of the estimable Mrs Sudbury while she's convalescing?' His smile slowly returned, pinching the sides of his mouth. 'You can't blame me for getting you wrong—you look far more like a golden nymph than a nurse. How do you get all that hair under a cap?'

'I manage,' Ruth said shortly. Suddenly his warm humour had a prickly edge to it, making her feel ill-at-ease. 'I've got to get back—nice meeting you. Bye.' But he didn't let her get far.

'Just a minute—' he caught up with her on the footpath. 'I can't let you walk out of my life like this. Sorry if I froze up on you just now, but that was just embarrassment. The Owens and I don't move in the same circles—as a matter of fact you may even be instructed not to speak to me—'

'Nobody tells me who I must or must not speak to!' Ruth broke in haughtily.

'No, not with that chin they wouldn't,' he conceded with another smile. 'Let me introduce myself. I'm Tony Graver, and that's my place down there.' He pointed to a tall white square building prominent at the far end of the bay just before the cliffs began to rise steeply again.

'Does everybody in Jersey live in large houses?' enquired Ruth, thinking of St Swithin Manor.

'That's not a house, it's a hotel—the Mirabelle—I'm the manager. Sorry I can't give you

one of my cards, I don't have a pocket on me.' The
warmth had returned to his voice. 'Could we meet
again—same time tomorrow? I'm out jogging every
morning. Perhaps you'd join me?'

'I don't think I'm up to jogging, just yet.' Ruth
didn't go into reasons. She hesitated, then thought,
why not? Her mother had urged her to enjoy herself
and get really fit again. This man looked the very
one to guide her to fitness, he exuded good health.
'All right,' she capitulated. 'See you tomorrow then,
and my name is Ruth—Ruth Richards.'

Up in the Prince's Room once more she stripped
out of her leisure-suit and put on a plain navy skirt
and white blouse. Nothing had been said to her
about wearing a uniform and she didn't know what
to do about her hair. She couldn't very well wear it
loose and she hadn't thought to bring a cap with
her. Coiling the plait round her head only made her
look like something out of an old Dutch masterpiece
and didn't suit her. Finally Ruth brushed out her
hair and swathed it into a chignon which she pinned
to the top of her head. The style flattered her and
gave her height and showed off to advantage her
slender neck. But she didn't feel fully dressed without
her cap.

As she had been told that breakfast was at eight
o'clock she had expected a formal meal served in
the dining-room. To her relief she found it a help
yourself affair in the kitchen. Pam was sitting at the
table alone and Ruth took a chair opposite her.

'Are we the only ones eating?' she enquired,
helping herself to coffee and toast.

'Dr Matt only has coffee which I take up to his
room, and Mrs Miller and Robbie have their breakfast in the old nursery,' Pam said as she put more
bread in the toaster.

'What about Dr Raynor?'

'Oh, she doesn't eat with us, she has her own self-contained flat in another part of the house. She only came down to dinner last night to keep you company. Dr Matt suggested it, he thought you might be feeling a bit strange, like.'

You can say that again, Ruth thought, remembering how Stephanie's presence had kept her tongue-tied throughout that nerve-racking meal, whereas without her she, Ruth, might have made some attempt at conversation. But she couldn't blame the glamorous Dr Raynor for that.

Pam crunched her toast with enjoyment. She was a buxom girl in her late teens, with a fair freckled skin and glorious auburn hair, but was by no means a beauty. She looked friendly and good-humoured, which she was.

'Sleep well, last night?' she asked as she poured Ruth another cup of coffee.

'I can't say I didn't sleep, but I didn't sleep comfortably—I don't see how anybody could in that room.'

'It isn't haunted, you know,' Pam chortled.

'Oh yes it is—it's haunted by all the babies who have been born there, and the girls who have languished for love there, and by old people who have died there. It's haunted by dreams and lost hopes and fears of the future—it ferments an atmosphere of days gone by, of intrigue and mystery and clandestine meetings—and I shouldn't be surprised if some high-ranking German officer didn't sleep there during the Occupation,' Ruth ended on a more practical note.

Pam stared at her open-mouthed. 'Wow! You've certainly got an imagination, haven't you!'

'So my mother is always telling me,' Ruth agreed,

then added earnestly, 'Pam, do me a favour—have
a word with Mrs Miller for me? See if you can
persuade her to give me another room—I don't mind
how small it is. I know it sounds ungrateful after
her doing me such a great favour, but—'

Pam gave a shout of laughter. 'It was no favour
to you, love. Mrs Miller only put you in that room
to spite Dr Raynor.' The girl squinted teasingly at
Ruth. 'It's true, cross my heart. Mrs Miller and Dr
Raynor are just like that—' and Pam crossed and
recrossed her two forefingers as if demonstrating a
fight with swords. 'Dr Raynor suggested that you
should have the use of her spare bedroom—and
immediately Mrs Miller jumped in with her idea of
the Prince's Room, and old Dr Owens always gives
in to Mrs Miller.'

'You sound as if you don't care for Mrs Miller
much,' said Ruth, surprised.

Pam didn't answer at first but after sizing up Ruth
with a certain shrewdness, she leant forward and
lowering her voice said, 'You didn't hear what I've
just said, understand? I've already lost one job this
summer for not keeping my big mouth shut, and I
don't want to lose this one too or I won't have any
money to take home in October.' Her ready smile
flashed into life again. 'But if that room really
worries you, I'll have a quiet word with Dr Raynor
about it and I'm sure she and Dr Matt will be able
to arrange something between them. Leave it to me,
love.' Which words of advice gave Ruth the
comfortable feeling that at least there was one
uncomplicated person living at St Swithin House.

Ruth was at her place at Mrs Sudbury's desk well
before nine o'clock and looked up expectantly when
the door opened. Stephanie Raynor walked in and
Ruth's heart sank—she knew she wasn't going to be

at her best with Dr Raynor, and her fears must have
shown on her face, for with a wry twist to her
mouth, Stephanie said, 'Don't worry, I'm not staying,
it's my day for the hospital. I only wanted to collect
my engagement book. Matt will be along shortly,
but I don't expect there will be any patients here
yet, it's a bit early for them.' There came the sound
of a door opening and closing and the shuffling of
feet, and Stephanie shrugged her shoulders. 'Come
back all I said, they *are* coming in early. No doubt
the news has got around and they want to give you
the once over.'

'Then they'll be disappointed—I'm nothing
special,' Ruth answered quickly.

Stephanie arched her shapely brows in surprise. 'I
believe you really meant that. Well, well, a modest
violet in our midst, that makes a nice change. But
don't cross yourself off so lightly, duckie, not with
those eyes.' She smiled unaffectedly. 'I suppose you
have a steady boy-friend at home?'

Ruth felt her cheeks go hot, she resented this
question. 'As a matter of fact I haven't, but I don't
see that it's any business of yours.'

The other woman looked slightly ashamed. 'It
isn't, and that was rude of me, I'm sorry. Well, if
there is anything I can do to help at any time, let
me know—'

She was almost out of the door before Ruth could
pluck up enough courage to say: 'You could do me
a favour. Pam was going to ask for me, but I feel I
should approach you myself. It's about sleeping
arrangements. Pam said something about you having
offered the use of your spare room, and I was
thinking—that is, if the offer still goes . . .' Ruth
floundered, distracted by the other woman's undis-

guised delight. 'That is, if it's convenient,' she added lamely.

'Oh, it's convenient.' Stephanie's brilliant eyes glinted mischievously. 'I don't blame you wanting to move from that musty brocade and satin mausoleum. I'll be back at lunchtime to take you up to my flat, but I warn you, the spare room is very small. Still, it's modern. Bye for now, I must skip,' and she went off, humming beneath her breath.

If she hadn't already been alerted by what Pam had said at breakfast, Ruth would have felt flattered by Stephanie's reaction to her request, but now Ruth knew that it was entirely due to Stephanie being able to score a point off Mrs Miller. Ruth gave a little moan and lowered her head in her hands. Oh, help, I hope you haven't stirred things up even more, she told herself. And was it wise of her to move into Stephanie's flat? She didn't really want to become too involved with her—not that Ruth disliked the other woman, but she didn't feel easy in her presence. Stephanie was a clever, sophisticated woman who made Ruth feel gauche and untried, and what was her relationship with Matt? There was a bond of some kind between them, one had only to be in their presence for a few minutes to detect that, and though Ruth knew that, what she had said to Stephanie about being none of her business applied to herself as well. She couldn't get speculation out of her mind, so it was a relief when her thoughts were broken into by the door opening a second time and this time it *was* Matt.

'Ah, you're here ready,' he said in his serious manner. 'Did you sleep well?'

'Yes, thank you.' Ruth wasn't going into that again.

'Good, well I see that the waiting-room is half-full already.' He took a memo pad from his pocket. 'Let me just check—there should be four patients referred from their last visit to my father. A case of varicose veins, a possible ganglion, a primigravida of twenty-four weeks, and an acute case of vertigo. They are all registered patients, which means they will recoup some of their expenses from the Health Scheme. Patients are not compelled to register with a particular doctor, so there may be some casuals calling in as well.'

'And visitors?' Ruth asked, thinking of the crowds of holiday-makers she had seen at the airport and in the towns they had driven through.

'Possibly—though emergencies usually go straight to hospital.' Matt gave her a grave, searching look. 'Are you feeling nervous?'

'No,' said Ruth untruthfully, aware that she was more nervous of his nearness than the thought of unknown patients.

His smile with its lingering sadness set her heart racing. If just by smiling at her like that he could reduce her to a quivering jelly, what would her condition be at the end of a morning working alongside him? 'Right you are then. Would you tell the first patient to come in, Nurse,' he said, as he made for his own room.

CHAPTER THREE

THE first three cases proved quite straightforward and presented no difficulties either to Matt or to Ruth.

The primigravida, a woman in her early twenties, was eagerly awaiting the birth of her first baby.

'Only three more months to go, it'll seem more like three years,' she confided cheerfully to Ruth as she was dressing after her examination. Her name was Sheila Cottle and she originally came from South London, but while on holiday in Jersey two summers previously she had met Marvin, the son of a local farmer, and after a whirlwind romance they had married.

'Fancy me a farmer's wife,' she giggled as Ruth laced up her shoes for her. 'My family said I wouldn't stick it, but I will, I love it here. I used to be nervous of cows but not the cows we have, the beautiful doe-eyed things.' She was blissfully happy, everything was wonderful to her—pregnancy gave her a bloom that gleamed in her eyes and her hair. Yet she still called London 'home' and spoke of it wistfully, Ruth thought.

The next two patients, Mrs Selby with varicose veins and Mr Loveday with a ganglion on the back of his wrist, were referred to hospital for further treatment, but Mrs Fraser, the elderly lady with the vertigo, posed more of a problem. Ruth stayed in her own room reading through the patient's notes while Matt saw to her.

Mrs Fraser had first called to see the elder Dr Owens just over a week previously. Her spell of dizziness had come on suddenly and for no apparent reason. Her husband had brought her a cup of tea in bed as usual and as she sat up to take it from him she had the sensation that the room was spinning around her. Her husband had made her stay in bed to see if the sensation would pass, but if anything her giddiness increased—even turning over in bed brought on further attacks.

Mrs Fraser was a highly-strung person with a nervous temperament and always fearful of being a nuisance to others. She refused to allow the doctor to be sent for, and insisted on getting up and getting dressed and calling on him instead.

Dr Matthew Owens had been unable to find any cause for the dizziness. The only clue he got was that Mrs Fraser had been on a boat trip to Guernsey the previous day, the sea had been rough and she had felt rather queasy, as she put it. Dr Owens had prescribed a sedative, advised her to rest as much as possible, and to call and see him or rather, his son, in a week's time.

Ruth had just finished reading this when Matt's light flashed on. She went in to him.

'I've sent Mrs Fraser along to the examination room,' he said. 'Would you go and help her off with her dress. I'd like to check her heart and take her blood pressure. It's sure to be up, with a woman of her disposition just the mere fact of visiting a surgery is enough to shoot her blood pressure sky-high.'

Matt was right, Mrs Fraser's blood pressure *was* high, but ten minutes later when she was sitting up and dressed, it had dropped considerably. Matt took Ruth on one side.

'There's nothing wrong with her heart,' he said

reassuringly. 'She has a good steady pulse. I'll prescribe something for her blood pressure, it's only mildly up now but it would be better to get it back to normal. I did wonder if her dizziness might have been brought on by wax in her ears but they are both clear. I'm beginning to think there is something in this seasickness idea.'

'You mean this dizziness she complains of is a latent form of seasickness?' Ruth queried.

'Something like that. That trip to Guernsey and back must have been rough enough to affect her balance of equilibrium, coupled by the fact that she suffers from catarrh and her Eustachian tubes are still partially blocked. That she's highly-strung could be another factor. She's still complaining of dizziness especially when she looks up or looks down or turns her head suddenly, though she says it's not as bad as it was. I'd like my father to keep a check on her, because of her labile blood pressure more than anything. Make an appointment for her to see him in early October. How many more patients are there?'

'Five, two others only called for renewed prescriptions.'

'Right, I'll see those and then I must be off on my rounds.' Matt's dark hazel eyes rested on her briefly, long enough to stir her senses, making her realise more than ever the depth of the impact he had made on her. 'While I'm out there are some letters you could be doing for me. Can you type?'

'Only with two fingers,' Ruth admitted reluctantly.

One side of his mouth went up in a slow smile. 'That's an improvement on Mrs Sudbury, she uses her thumbs,' he said, 'and if you require any correction fluid you'll find a bottle in the cupboard.' Ruth could tell by his voice that he was trying to be facetious, and she could tell too that he was sadly out of practice—the words were too contrived. Her throat constricted with sympathy and she was ashamed that for a time yesterday she had felt antagonistic towards him. He looked a man who had suffered—was still suffering—and being flippant didn't come easily to him.

Ruth watched from the window as he drove off in the sleek expensive car that had brought her from the airport. That he did not lack money was obvious, but he did not lack wretchedness either and one did not make up for the other.

Mid-morning brought Pam along with a cup of coffee for her, and following close behind, practically clinging to her skirts, was Robbie. He eyed Ruth owlishly with unfathomable toffee-brown eyes.

'Do you mind company, love?' Pam asked. 'It's something Mrs Sudbury started when Robbie was a toddler. She used to keep an eye on him when his moth-' Pam hesitated, then went on chirpily, 'He's no bother, he just likes to sit and do his crayoning and drink his milk or orange-juice. I think you'll find Mrs Sudbury keeps some biscuits in a tin in her desk.'

Pam went off leaving Ruth and the silent boy to become acquainted. Ruth offered him a biscuit and gravely Robbie helped himself then settled at a table with his drink and colouring book. Ruth thoughtfully stirred her coffee, wondering what it was Pam had left unsaid. She looked across at the child now engrossed in his crayoning, his head slightly on one side, his long fair lashes screening his unusual eyes. In repose the strained, wary look on his face was less in evidence and Ruth tried to imagine him smiling, his thin little face lighting up with boyish glee, but it was beyond her—the first time that she could remember her imagination not functioning. She wanted so much to get some reaction from the boy. She was always at her best with children because in some ways she was still very much a child at heart herself, but she knew that if she tried to approach him or to cuddle him, he would panic and run away. The barrier of silence around the boy was as impenetrable as a barbed wire fence.

'Robbie,' she said softly, and she knew that he heard because of the sudden tension in his posture, but he went on with his crayoning as if she hadn't spoken.

'Robbie,' she said again. 'Can you swim?'

There was a slight hesitation and then he nodded, but he still didn't look at her.

'Oh good, I was hoping someone would help me to swim properly—I'm not very good at it, I splash too much and don't like getting my face wet.' Ruth lied glibly, not that she considered herself lying—just using a little diplomacy in order to arouse a child's interest.

Robbie *was* interested, she saw a questioning look flicker in and out of his eyes, then he nodded and she took that to mean he was willing to teach her to swim. 'You can always get to a man through his ego,' her mother had once said to her, and now she smiled at the thought. To her astonishment Robbie smiled back. It was a very fleeting smile, if she had blinked then she would have missed it, and the next moment the child was back to his colouring. But Ruth felt she had made an important breakthrough and didn't intend to push her luck by trying to go any further that morning.

The letters were finished and Ruth had dealt with several phone calls when the clock on the wall chimed midday. As if it were a signal, Robbie collected his work together and shortly afterwards Mrs Miller came in for him.

Ruth could tell there was something wrong by the look of martyrdom on the housekeeper's round plump face. The pale eyes, enlarged behind the thick glasses, were full of reproach, and Ruth thought she saw what was suspiciously like tears. 'I thought I could trust you,' the housekeeper murmured as she went past. 'I took to you, I really did. I thought what a nice, sweet-natured girl you were,' came a sigh from the depths of her heart, and Ruth watched with disbelief as a tear plopped straight from her eye on to her ample front. 'It hurts to find one's trust has been misplaced.' She could not quite meet Ruth's incredulous gaze. Robbie was waiting and she took his hand. 'Come along, dear. We mustn't make ourselves a nuisance to Nurse any longer.' Her voice quivered self-righteously.

Even the way she swept out of the room was a rebuke in itself. Ruth stared after her, feeling just as Mrs Miller had intended her to feel—guilty and remorseful. All this fuss over a change of room, for it was obvious this was what it was about—but was it worth all this emotional anguish! Ruth wished to goodness that she hadn't said anything about the beastly room. The last thing she wanted to do was hurt anybody's feelings though she couldn't help thinking that Mrs Miller's feelings were very easily hurt. She was either ultra-sensitive or just showing her annoyance in a more devious way. Ruth pushed that idea away, even reproached herself for thinking it. She liked Mrs Miller, and she could tell that little Robbie adored her. She had once been told that children and animals were never wrong about people—that was good enough for Ruth.

Ruth's next battle with her conscience took place with the reappearance of Matt Owens. She heard the car swish up the drive, the door slam, the front door open and then his firm tread in the hall. It struck her afresh how lithe and athletic his build was as he came swinging into the room. He frowned at seeing her as if he had forgotten her existence, then his face cleared.

'How have you got on? Any problems?' he asked in his abrupt but not uncivil manner.

She showed him the list of appointments she had made and handed him the typed letters. He nodded, agreeing them, then looked directly at her, not through her as he had previously.

'I expect you'd like a breath of fresh air after being cooped up here all morning. There's still half an hour till lunchtime—would you like to explore the grounds? I'll show you a way through the pine woods down to the cliffs.'

Hesitantly Ruth explained that she had been up early enough that morning to go exploring and had found her way to the sea. This information seemed to please him, his hazel eyes flashed her a look that was full of speculation. They were remarkable eyes, darker than his small son's and rimmed with gold. Ruth suddenly realised she was staring right into them, could even see miniature portraits of herself in each pupil, and overcome with confusion she hastily started to tidy a desk that didn't need tidying, fearing that her flaming cheeks might betray her.

Perhaps Matt hadn't noticed or if he did attached no significance to it, for there was no change in his voice as he asked, 'Did you look westwards towards the bay? That small settlement is the oldest part of St Swithin. Hundreds of years ago it was a thriving little fishing village, now it's an unspoilt holiday resort—or rather, was unspoilt until that monstrous concrete and glass eyesore was erected,' he added, his voice taking on a bitter edge.

'You mean the Mirabelle?' Ruth said, not suspecting the trap she was laying for herself.

The light went out of his eyes—they turned opaque and hard.

'What do you know about the Mirabelle?' His tone was a warning, but still unsuspecting Ruth went on to explain about her meeting with Tony Graver who had introduced himself as the manager of the new hotel. Only then did she notice the danger signals in Matt's face, the narrowing of the eyes and the fierce throbbing of a nerve in his lean cheek. Her voice petered out and she stood there nervously, sensing an undercurrent of tension in the man opposite that was like a coiled spring ready to snap.

'You actually spoke to that chap Graver?' he rapped at her.

'We just happened to meet on the cliffs, it seemed a normal thing to do.' She didn't add that she had half-promised to meet the man again the next morning, it didn't seem politic at the moment.

'Did you tell him who you were?'

'Yes.' Ruth recalled now Tony's reaction, his whimsical half-smile when he had said: 'The Owens and I don't move in the same circles—as a matter of fact you may even be instructed not to speak to me—'

She hadn't believed him and she could hardly believe her ears now when Matt did just that. 'You will oblige me in future by not having anything to do with that man,' he said fiercely.

'I—I shall speak to whoever I want—' she spluttered indignantly.

'Not while you're under my roof!'

'I shan't be meeting him under *your* roof!' Ruth flung back at him. 'And who I care to meet outside is entirely my business and has nothing to do with you!'

They faced each other across the desk—wide blue eyes and narrowed hazel ones equally wrathful. But under his seething anger Matt could not ignore a grudging admiration for the spirited girl opposite. At first sight he had taken her for a demure, pretty little thing but with not much going for her. He felt now that he had been hoodwinked by her dimples and chocolate-box prettiness—that under her cuddlesome appearance was a thin rod of determination. His anger flared anew. How dare some unknown little chit like this come into his home and cause disruption—he could have shaken her! He marched round the desk with that in mind, but when he got near and saw the slight trembling of her soft upper lip, felt the warmth of her body that exuded the faint perfume of lilies-of-the-valley, a sudden reawakening of old longings swept over him and he took her roughly in his arms and crushed his lips upon hers.

Then he released her and stood back, staring at her with steady eyes, his feelings masked by an impassive expression. 'Let that be a lesson to you,' he said stonily, and walked out.

Ruth put her fingers to her lips which still tingled from the pressure he had exerted. She waited for her sense of unreality to wear of—for feelings of indignation and humiliation to sweep over her—but the only feelings she had were ones of wonder and curiosity. Wonder that a man like Matt Owens had suddenly gone against his better judgment, and curiosity as to why, when he had obviously wanted to hit her, he had kissed her instead.

As Ruth passed the dining-room on her way upstairs to tidy up for lunch she met Pam with a laden tray. As she came nearer Pam said: 'Sorry I let slip about you wanting to change your room. Hope Ma Miller didn't show the dent in her feelings too obviously.'

'She went over the top,' Ruth replied ruefully.

Pam grinned. 'You'll get hardened to that in a day or two. Don't worry, she'll soon get over it. Happy lunchtime!' and she went on her way, blissfully unaware that the lunchtime for Ruth was to prove anything but happy.

In the sanctuary of the Prince's Room Ruth flopped down on the high bed and tried to sort out the tangled knot in her mind. She was still shaken by the way Matt had kissed her, and dreaded having to meet him at the dining-table. She hoped Stephanie would be there to ease the strain, otherwise the situation would be unendurable.

If he had kissed her from a sudden impulse, or because he had found her irresistible, Ruth wouldn't have given the episode another thought. It had happened to her before. The young housemen of St Catherine's had once voted her the most kissable nurse of her year and she had had to spend weeks afterwards putting them in their place. But Matt's kiss hadn't been like that—it hadn't lacked passion but it had been a cold calculated passion that was worse than a blow. Perhaps after all he had been wanting to teach her a lesson in humility, and that thought put her back up. She'd show him that she wasn't just a temporary distraction he could vent his feelings on. He'd soon learn that she had a mind of own!

Lunch turned out to be as nerve-racking as she had expected. Stephanie was present, but then so was the housekeeper which evened things out.

Throughout the meal, Mrs Miller sat in the martyred silence of one whose self-esteem had been wounded, but Matt's stony silence was more aggressive, and when reaching for the salad bowl he knocked over a glass of water he swore irritably below his breath. Stephanie looked at Ruth with raised eyebrows; it was obvious that she thought there had been some difference of opinion between the other two which went even further towards undermining Ruth's peace of mind, knowing she would have to explain later.

The opportunity came when she was taken upstairs to see Stephanie's flat. For a self-contained apartment it had everything—a modern kitchen and bathroom, large living-room, and a double and a single bedroom. The second bedroom was small with a corner window overlooking the courtyard, but what it lacked in a view it made up for by its fresh and up-to-date furnishings. After the heavy brocades and velvets of the state room it appeared to Ruth's eyes as crisp and refreshing as a spring morning.

'There's a built-in cupboard large enough to take your suitcase and shoes as well as clothes, and the dressing-table turns down and converts into a writing-desk—' Stephanie demonstrated this. 'I'm sorry the room looks so bare,' she added, 'but I expect you have a few personal trinkets you'll want to spread around.'

'I think it's just right, I don't like a lot of clutter —perhaps some flowers,' Ruth suggested.

'Help yourself from the garden, we all do—there's fruit too, buckets of it, so don't be reluctant to take all you want. Now I'd better show you where things are kept in the kitchen.'

The kitchen had a small dining area furnished with a round stripped pine table and matching chairs. 'I eat here, except for lunch,' Stephanie explained. 'I have that at the hospital or downstairs with the others, it saves time. You're welcome to have breakfast here and your evening meal too, if it would suit you better.'

'Oh, it would suit me,' answered Ruth vehemently.

Stephanie laughed. She had loosened her honey-blonde hair and shaken it free, and hanging casually to her shoulders as it was now it suited her, made her look younger and softened the contours of her face. 'I guess you sensed the atmosphere at luncheon,' she said shrewdly. 'I hope you didn't think it had anything to do with you. I expect Matt had said something to hurt Mrs Miller's feelings, it happens all the time.'

'It had everything to do with me,' Ruth put in quickly, glad to get it off her chest. 'I was the one to upset Mrs Miller and then I upset Dr Owens. Oh dear, I hope you don't mind me saying this, Dr Raynor, but everybody in this house seems to be suffering from some form of neurosis—except Pam, she seems normal enough.'

Stephanie laughed again, a quiet chortle. 'Am I included with Pam or the others?'

'With Pam of course, there's no question about that.'

Ruth had meant this sincerely, but Stephanie gave her a hard look. 'I think you'll change your mind when you know me better,' she said, her eyes clouding. 'I think we all have something to hide, don't you? None of us goes about advertising what we really feel—we put a face on things. In my case it can be a very cool face. I don't think you took to me at first, did you?'

Not expecting such a personal query Ruth was caught off her guard and began to stammer out a denial which only made Stephanie grimace ruefully.

'Forget it,' she said. 'I didn't expect an answer, anyway. Now tell me how you managed to upset Matt? I can guess what caused Mrs Miller's look of martyrdom, but I'm puzzled about Matt. What went wrong this morning—some disagreement over a patient?'

'I wouldn't question a doctor's verdict on a patient, I'm not experienced enough for that.' Ruth sounded shocked. 'No—I just happened to mention the name Tony Graver, that's all.'

'Oh my God—that's all!' Stephanie mimicked in a tone of mock despair. She pulled out one of the chairs and sat down, motioning Ruth to sit opposite. 'We don't mention that name in this house—don't ask me why, I don't know the full story. I've only been here two years and the trouble goes back before then. I believe it's something to do with building that hotel. Both Dr Owens and Matt were dead against it, but the District Council voted them down. Believe me, Ruth, the name Tony Graver is like a red rag to a bull to Matt.'

Ruth felt that Stephanie wasn't telling the whole truth, that there was something else she knew that she wasn't at liberty to or didn't want to divulge. She seemed a bit edgy and avoided looking straight at Ruth. For her part Ruth felt that it was all a storm in a teacup, just as Mrs Miller taking umbrage at Ruth's move to another room was a storm in a—well, by comparison, a storm in an eggcup! Ruth felt she had been right in her verdict of neurosis as the common malady at St Swithin House, and she also felt that four weeks in this environment might have some effect on *her* psyche. There was something else she had to get off her mind too.

'I looked after little Robbie for a while this morning,' she said. 'I can't accept his disability lightly, I think it's criminal not to try to cure him of his speechlessness. With a father and a grandfather both doctors and the best medical treatment available to him, just to accept seems all wrong. They haven't given up hope that he will ever speak again, have they?' Ruth spoke passionately, her cheeks flushed and her eyes alight with fervour.

Stephanie's face took on a sober, rather pinched look and she began to drum nervously on the table with her fingers.

'Ruth, don't get me wrong if I remind you that just this minute you used the expression that you were not an experienced nurse. I want you to remember that when dealing with Robbie. This is something beyond your understanding, and you'd have to know the full story before you could begin to comprehend. Robbie's loss of speech is not just a physical thing, it's also a defect of the mind. Don't you think Matt and his father haven't done everything they can to find a cure? Matt has taken his boy to specialists in London and New York—every available test was tried out until it became plain they were causing more harm than good. They were driving the boy even more into his own private world, and it was then Matt decided to give up and let nature take its course. But you mustn't think he's indifferent; it was a real sacrifice for him to leave the boy here in Jersey when he took up the post as micro-biologist in London. He thought it would be better if Robbie stayed here among people he knew. This is the only home Robbie has known—he was born here.' Stephanie paused, looking down at her restless hands before she tucked them out of sight under the table. Ruth felt she had been on the point of mentioning Robbie's mother but had thought better of it. That subject, like the name of Tony

Graver, seemed also to be taboo.

There was a brief silence and Ruth decided to introduce a more mundane subject. 'You must let me pay you something towards my keep,' she said, which caused Stephanie to lift her head sharply.

'Certainly not, there's no question of that. When I joined the practice this rent-free flat was part of the deal. I believe your temporary post here includes your board? Well then, how can I possibly charge you. If you really want to do me a favour you can cook the meal occasionally. I loathe cooking.'

They sealed the bargain with a glass of sherry, and Ruth made a secret pact with herself that not only would she do the cooking but she would also buy some of the necessary provisions. Dr Owens was paying her well, she could afford it, and part of her was still reluctant to be under any obligation to this other woman. Though she liked Stephanie better now than on their first meeting, Ruth still felt a certain reservation towards her. But if it had been Pam who had the rent-free flat and offered to share it with her she would have had no such reservations.

It was a relief to Ruth to find when she returned to the surgery for the afternoon session that Stephanie was in charge, Matt having taken the afternoon off, so once more the dreaded encounter with him was postponed for another occasion. Stephanie took longer than Matt to get through each case, not because she was a slower worker, but knowing most of the patients personally she spent some time chatting to them. Ruth realised that this could be as effective as a tonic, and it was something she often regretted she didn't have time for at St Catherine's.

There was a girl waiting to see the doctor who had aroused Ruth's interest, perhaps because of her unusual beauty. She was only about sixteen with a pale olive complexion and dark eyes and hair, and reminded Ruth of a painting of the Madonna she had once seen in an old master. Even though it was a warm day she had on a loose coat that reached almost to her ankles, and she clutched it around herself as if she was feeling the cold.

Ruth knew that the young did not conform to fashion, or rather, the way-out clothes they sported were in a way a fashion in their own right, but it did cross her mind that the girl might be feeling the cold through a thyroid deficiency or perhaps anaemia. Ruth knew all about that having been through it herself, and remembered how cold she used to feel before her treatment. The girl had the same listless look about her too.

Stephanie's light flashed on and when Ruth entered her room she found her trying to comfort a middle-aged woman who was crying silently into her handkerchief; she was a short, stocky little person and was slumped down in the chair as if all the stuffing had been shaken out of her.

Stephanie looked up at Ruth and said softly, 'Nurse, would you make Mrs Mack a cup of tea. Take her along to your room and let her rest for a while, she's had a bit of a shock.'

'I'm all right now,' said the woman shakily. 'And it's not really a shock. I should have come to you before, but I kept putting it off.' She allowed Ruth to lead her away, leaning heavily on her arm. The girl, the only patient now waiting, looked up startled at their appearance and as she moved her coat fell open. It was then that Ruth noticed she was well advanced in pregnancy. That was something she hadn't thought of she told herself ruefully—the most natural thing of all had eluded her.

A cup of tea seemed to revive Mrs Mack, she even looked a bit guilty as she refused a refill. 'I should have come sooner,' she said soberly. 'As soon as I noticed the lump—here,' she dabbed cautiously at her breast. 'But I couldn't face being told what I already knew in my heart. I had the silly idea that if I ignored it it might go away, but of course it didn't.' Her eyes welled again and she scrubbed at them furiously. 'Dr Raynor is making an appointment for me at the hospital, she said I'll have to have a—a—' Mrs Mack had either forgotten the word or else couldn't bring herself to mention it.

'Biopsy,' Ruth prompted gently. 'You mustn't worry about that.' She took a seat beside Mrs Mack and put a comforting hand on her arm. 'All it means is that a small piece of tissue will be removed from the lump and then studied under the microscope in order to find out whether the lump is benign or malignant. Would it help you to know that my own mother had that done about eight years ago and she went through the same fears and worries that you are going through now, and she could have spared herself, for the lump proved non-malignant. It was removed successfully and she's had no bother since.'

Mrs Mack squeezed Ruth's hand and gave a faint smile. 'But I still have to face the fact that I might not be so lucky—that my lump may prove malignant.' She put her empty cup on the table, and stood up. 'Thank you for that tea dear, it was very welcome. Now I must go home and break the news to my husband. I didn't even let on that I was coming to see the doctor today because he's such an old worry-guts.'

Ruth had left her door partly open. She had been too occupied with Mrs Mack to notice that Matt had passed by a few minutes previously. He had stopped, hearing her voice, and had listened for a while before going on to his own room opposite. There he sat on the edge of his desk brooding over what he had heard. He opened his door a few inches and saw Ruth escorting the patient to the entrance—their voices carried.

'I know it's easy for me to say don't worry, but I will say it all the same,' Ruth was telling Mrs Mack. 'Even if the news is bad, it's not the end. Cancer can be cured, you know. I work in a large London hospital—I've seen patients getting well after treatment, there's so much can be done for them these days apart from surgery. There's radiotherapy and chemotherapy, and I do think the state of one's of mind is important too. I mean, you mustn't give in—you must fight back—tell yourself you're going to get well.' Ruth was so earnest, her eyes and voice eloquent with sincerity, that nobody could have taken offence, least of all Mrs Mack who would have grasped reassurance from any quarter. 'I know I haven't been a nurse very long,' Ruth went on, 'but during that time, at the hospital, I've seen that if patients are determined to get better, they usually do. It is so essential not to give in, to tell yourself that you're going to conquer it.' Ruth broke off suddenly and a self-conscious smile flickered across her face. 'I expect you think I'm too young to know what I'm talking about, but I'm not as young as I look. And I'm not trying to lecture you, please don't think that.'

Mrs Mack patted Ruth's hand. 'Of course you're not lecturing me, I know that—and I know just what you're trying to do. You're trying to reassure me, you dear sweet child. God bless you, Nurse, I'm very grateful to you,' and all at once she leant forward and kissed Ruth on her cheek.

She had gone before Ruth had recovered from her surprise. Two unexpected kisses in one day—but what a difference between them! It was then Ruth noticed that Matt was standing in the doorway of his room, looking at her in a way that sent the colour flooding her face.

He came up to her. 'That was a nice tribute and well deserved,' he said gravely. 'I apologise for any doubts I had about you being suitable for this job, and I also apologise for—' but Ruth wasn't to find out the reason for the second apology just then, for Stephanie came out of her room and interrupted.

'Wasn't there another patient waiting to see me?' she asked Ruth. 'A girl in a long coat. Not one of my regulars, she must have been a visitor.'

Ruth looked surprised. 'I thought she was in with you as she wasn't in the waiting-room when I showed Mrs Mack out.'

Stephanie seemed unconcerned. 'Not to worry, she'll be back if it's important.' She turned smilingly to Matt, slipping her arm through his. 'Have you got a moment to spare, I want some advice. No, nothing to do with work, something private,' and she gave one of her characteristic low chuckles.

They went into Matt's room, heads together, talking quietly. A closeness more than physical, more than professional seemed to unite them, and the door closing behind them, shutting Ruth out, did more than anything else to remind her that she was just a temporary stand-in.

CHAPTER FOUR

RUTH did not keep her appointment with Tony Graver the following morning after all, and for two very good reasons.

Firstly, she overslept; secondly, even before going to bed she had decided not to go jogging with Tony. Not because of Matt's attitude, but rather because of a belated sense of loyalty towards him. He had revealed something of his secret self in that long meditative look he had cast at her, and she knew he was ashamed of his behaviour. He had been on the point of apologising for that contemptuous kiss when Stephanie had interrupted. Ruth saw no sense in adding to tensions already at work in the house, and it mattered little to her whether she saw Tony again or not.

Matt came into her dream that night and weird and unreal as it was, it stayed in her mind for days afterwards. In the dream she found herself hurrying through the pine woods, the tall black trees like spectral shapes appearing and disappearing in a swirling mist. Ruth didn't know why she was hurrying, only that there was some sense of urgency. The murmur of the sea came from far away as if the mist was soaking up sound as well as distance, but when at last she was free of the trees it grew louder in volume and swelled into a noise like thunder, and at the same time the mist cleared and she saw the figure of a man standing on the cliff edge. She thought 'There's Tony, I must tell him I can't come jogging after all,' and started towards him, but just then the figure turned and it wasn't Tony, it was Matt. He gave her a look which seemed to say 'Keep away from me, leave me alone,' then the mist closed in on him again, blotting him out of sight. A sense of imminent danger filled Ruth and she tried to shout out a warning, but though she knew she was shrieking at the top of her voice, warning Matt against falling over the cliff, no sound came out when she opened her mouth. And when she tried to run to him, her feet felt as if they were nailed to the ground. She made one last effort, and suddenly she was free, and she began to run. The mist cleared, but there was no figure standing on the cliff edge and when she looked down all she could see was the jutting cave below with its cruel jagged edges. In her dream it looked even more menacing than it had in reality. She fancied it was trap for unwary travellers, that it concealed dark secrets in its sinister depths. The conviction grew on her that Matt had either slipped or thrown himself off the cliff edge and was lying injured or dead in the black abyss, and she heard herself screaming out above the cry of the gulls—'Matt—Matt . . .'—and that was when she woke, her heart pounding and a feeling of suffocation gripping her throat.

The luminous hands on her bedside clock showed four o'clock. Ruth sipped from her glass of water and lay down again waiting for her heart to stop its wild beating. She felt hot and threw off the duvet and tried to compose herself for sleep, but instead lay tossing wondering what the dream meant—whether there was any connection between Matt and the cave, her imagination at work even at this time of the morning. Finally she drifted off to sleep and knew nothing more until Stephanie came

into her room with a cup of tea. It was nearly eight
o'clock!

With heavy-lidded eyes Ruth struggled into a
sitting position and took the cup. 'I'm sorry, Dr
Raynor, I didn't mean to oversleep,' she apologised.
'I forgot to put on my alarm.'

'We're not late, and breakfast is ready any time
you are. I let you sleep on—you had a disturbed
night.' Stephanie wore a faintly whimsical smile.
'You obviously had a nightmare because you cried
out something in your sleep. I came across and
listened outside your door, but it was all quiet so I
guessed you'd gone off again. I hope we didn't
overwork you yesterday.'

Momentarily, Ruth had forgotten her dream but
now it came back to her with startling clarity and
she hoped it wasn't Matt's name she had shouted in
her sleep—if so, that could account for a certain
archness in Stephanie's smile. Coupled to that
discomfiture was the feeling that it wasn't right for
her to be waited on like this, rather the other way
round. She started to say she was the one who
should have got up and made tea, but Stephanie
didn't let her finish.

'Oh nonsense—we'll take it in turns if that would
make you feel better, and less of the Dr Raynor if
you please. It makes me feel old enough to be your
mother the way you say it! I won't be in for lunch
by the way. It's my day off and I'm going to visit
some friends in St Helier. I might even stay the
night. You'll be all right?'

Ruth noticed then that Stephanie was already
dressed for going out, wearing a plain navy-blue
cotton suit with an emerald green motif on the lapels
and cuffs, and shoes of a similiar green. She gave an
impression of stylised elegance, and the fragrance of

her expensive French perfume lingered on after she
had left. Ruth sighed as she hopped out of bed.
She'd never look like that in a hundred years—to
start with she hadn't got the figure. But she couldn't
help wondering if there was another man in Stephanie's life, and felt quite uplifted at the idea.

Stephanie had borrowed a cap from the hospital
for Ruth, and worn with her white blouse and navy
skirt it gave her the look of being in uniform, and
being in uniform made her feel more up to the job.
Before leaving her room Ruth straightened the bed
and opened the window wide to let in the early
morning sun. Mrs Miller was in the courtyard
watering some geraniums in a tub. She looked up,
and seeing Ruth she smiled and gave a cheery wave
of the hand. You're in favour again, Ruth told
herself joyfully. She hadn't liked being at odds with
the housekeeper and it was with a light heart that
she went down to open the surgery.

By chance she met Mrs Miller in the hall—or was
it by chance? The housekeeper stopped her, she was
smiling still. 'I'm sorry I was a bit offhand with you
yesterday,' she said unctuously. 'I realise now it
wasn't your fault, you must have been got at by
others. I knew you wouldn't turn on me—I can
always judge my instincts, and I knew you're not
the type of girl to be underhand or go behind
anybody's back and say unkind things about them.'
She edged as near as her ample bosom allowed,
lowering her voice. 'Don't believe all you hear about
me, my dear. There's some in this place would like
to see the back of me and they don't care how they
go about it. They'll work on you if they think they
can make an ally of you, so just a gentle warning,
dear.' And with another smile and a nod she went
on her way, having successfully turned Ruth's light-

heartedness inside out.

'They' of course meant Matt and Stephanie, they were the only two in the house who could be clubbed together as a pair, and now Mrs Miller had successfully made Ruth feel like the one in the middle—a buffer between them and the housekeeper—which could lead to all kinds of complications.

It was a ridiculous situation and Ruth was annoyed with herself for attaching any importance to it. What had Matt called her that first day—a bird of passage? Right, that's what she'd be then, a bird of passage doing her job well and flying back home when it was done.

The dreaded encounter with Matt passed off without difficulty. He was in a very professional mood this morning. Gone was the brooding look and long periods of retrospective silence, though even under his efficient and matter-of-fact manner the melancholy showed through. He made one brief reference to their clash of wills the day before, saying in a casual but contrived way, 'I apologise for my behaviour yesterday. It was quite out of character, I don't make a habit of pouncing on unsuspecting girls and kissing them. I give you leave to slap my face now if you like.'

His rather pathetic attempt at humour kindled Ruth's compassion; it showed her how out of practice he was in showing levity. There were no laughter lines stamped on his handsome gaunt features, only lines of suffering. Someone, somehow, in the past had hurt him very deeply and it showed.

'I'd rather just forget the whole matter,' she answered with the same false lightness with which he had introduced the subject, and felt rather than saw his sense of relief. That, for the present, was the last word on the matter for within minutes they were absorbed in the work in hand.

Ruth had learned her lesson from yesterday and she meticulously took the name of every patient waiting to see the doctor. She realised she had slipped up by not getting the necessary information from the pregnant teenager, but neither Stephanie nor Matt had rebuked her. She felt they had agreed to overlook it because it was her first day and the duties were new to her, but that was no excuse really. Common sense should have told her that the first thing to do was to check off the name of patients but, as Ruth would have been the first one to admit, common sense wasn't her forte.

All morning she waited for the girl to make a reappearance and when she didn't Ruth wondered if she had gone to see another doctor instead, not that she had time to spare speculating about one particular patient, as there were so many others to attend to that morning. None of them taxed her abilities, and only once did she have to call Matt to her aid, and that was when she couldn't get the electronic sphygmomanometer to work. She had forgotten to switch it on! Matt didn't say anything—he didn't even give her one of his black looks which showed how hard he was trying to keep their relationship on an even keel, but the patient collapsed in giggles.

Ruth started off on the wrong foot with the next patient, Mrs Mann.

She was a thin, well-dressed, overmade-up woman in her early sixties, with black hair liberally sprinkled with grey. She was reading a copy of a glossy magazine when Ruth approached. 'May I have your name, please?' Ruth asked, ready to check it off in the appointment book if it was there, if not, to note it down.

The woman stared coldly at Ruth over the top of the magazine. 'I have been coming here long enough for my name to be quite well known,' she said imperiously, but with difficulty as her breathing was so laboured. Each breath she took made a rasping noise in her chest. Ruth was reluctant to insist, seeing that talking was such an effort, but she was able to describe her quite accurately to Matt and he recognised the patient at once.

'That's Mrs Mann, I attended her the last time I was doing a locum for my father. When she was my age she was a chain-smoker, now she's paying the price. Show her in.' He sounded angry.

Mrs Mann was the last patient of the morning. When she had gone Matt came into Ruth's room to give her some notes. 'You can add these to Mrs Mann's record card. Has she made another appointment?' he asked.

'Yes, in a month's time to see your father.'

He smiled grimly. 'She doesn't like me, she finds me too abrasive, and I've told her one or two home truths in the past. She can't understand why we can't promise her a cure, but what she is suffering from is incurable. Do you know anything about emphysema? Do you remember it from your textbooks?'

Ruth might have done if he hadn't looked at her with that unblinking stare. Now her mind went blank. 'Is that the trouble with poor Mrs Mann?' she asked.

Matt smiled faintly at the word 'poor'—it showed where Ruth's sympathies lay. He began to prowl restlessly about the room, his tall lean frame moving with the grace and suppleness of a panther. 'Yes, that's the trouble with Mrs Mann,' he repeated, crisply. 'Her lungs have lost their elasticity and are

in a constant state of inflation so she has great
difficulty in exhaling. She gave up smoking five years
ago, but by then it was twenty years too late. Do
you smoke?' The question came out unexpectedly.

'I've never had the urge to try,' Ruth said. She
hoped she didn't sound smug, but Matt seemed
satisfied with her answer.

'Good, because Jersey is a paradise for smokers.
There's no tax on tobacco here, so cigarettes are dirt
cheap. That doesn't mean that every islander is an
inveterate smoker, though I suppose like everywhere
else there are exceptions. It's the visitors that go
mad—some of them buy up cigarettes as if their
lives depended on them, when in fact the reverse is
true. I've even heard some holiday-makers admit
that they don't smoke at home because they can't
afford to. Well, they certainly make up for it when
they come here!' He gave a mirthless laugh and a
slow, tired smile lightened his face for a moment.
His voice, when he spoke again, was less strident. 'I
mustn't get on my hobby-horse—I'm not here as a
judge but a healer, not that I can heal Mrs
Mann . . .'

'Is there nothing you can do for her?' asked Ruth
in the pause that followed.

'Yes, I can send her to the chest clinic for treatment in Intermittent Positive Pressure Breathing or
I can precribe a bronchodilator aerosol, or I can
give her drugs to loosen the bronchial phlegm. What
I can't do is repair her lungs.' Matt went over to the
window and stared out at the circular drive. Standing
in that position he recalled to Ruth the figure in her
dream, and the same feeling of imminent danger
came over her. She began to tidy her notes with
nervous fingers and Matt turned, consulting his
watch at the same time.

'It's lunchtime. Are you eating with us today?' One eyebrow went up enquiringly.

'I'm skipping lunch today,' Ruth explained. 'I had a good breakfast and I'm not hungry. I thought I'd take a walk down to the bay and back.' Matt didn't believe her, he thought she had an appointment with Tony Graver. He didn't say anything but disappointment and disapproval clouded his face. 'Be back at two sharp,' he said abruptly, and left.

The man's impossible, Ruth told herself, he didn't even give me a chance to explain I only wanted a walk. But then, why should she have to explain her every move to him! Upstairs in her room she took off her cap and shook her hair loose. That was better—she felt freer now. She didn't have time to change, just slipped on a lightweight anorak over her blouse, then ran hurriedly down the stairs and through the kitchen. Pam was there, alone, preparing a chopped salad. Homemade soup, bread, cheese and salad was the usual lunch at St Swithin House.

Ruth explained that she was not staying for lunch but going for a walk instead, but Pam would insist on giving her some biscuits and an apple 'to tide you over'. Pam had a healthy teenage appetite herself and couldn't understand anyone missing a meal from choice.

Nothing could be as different from the pine woods of her dream as the graceful trees through which Ruth made her way down towards the cliffs now. Instead of swirling mist there were pools of dappled sunshine; instead of a sense of impending doom the sweet scent of the heliotropes in the flower-beds wafted up to her. Ruth could afford to laugh at her morbid fancies now—how could she have believed anything sinister was connected with these lovely surroundings? The sun had brought out the perfume

of other flowers too, petunias and carnations and
the delicate nerines, the Jersey lilies that grew as
prolifically as weeds. Magpies scolded sleepily from
the tree tops and squirrels scurried out of sight as
she approached. It was a beautiful mellow September
afternoon and already Ruth felt that Jersey was
doing her good. It was early days yet to be sure, but
the feeling of listlessness that had dogged her for
months seemed to be lessening. She was still taking
her iron tablets, but she hoped that by the end of
the month even they would be things of the past.
Not that she wanted to dwell too much on what was
likely to happen by the end of the month. She would
be back in England then and she was reluctant to
think of that. She had only been in Jersey two days
and she was already under its spell.

The same sense of tranquillity went with her all
the way to the cliff-top path. There was hardly any
wind and the sea spread inert like a sheet of blue
shot silk threaded with silver strands. A shimmering
heat haze made a range of distant cliffs seem like a
mirage floating a few feet above the still waters.

Ruth walked over to the edge of the cliff and
looked down. The cave yawned just below her and
again she wondered how she could have kidded
herself there was anything sinister about it; it wasn't
even a true cave, only a deep cleft in the cliff face.
Certainly anybody falling into it could be killed, but
then so would anybody falling on to the jagged
rocks beneath. Ruth drew back as her old phobia
about heights took hold of her. She looked at her
watch, if she hurried she could get as far as the bay
and back. All she had seen of Jersey so far was from
the windows of Matt's car and she wanted more
information than that to send to her mother.

Though in places the incline was quite steep, Ruth

found the walk easy. Spreading away on her right
was a great carpet of heather, colourful swathes of
purple and pink flowers, a delight to the senses.
Ruth had never seen anything to match it before or
realised that in the mass heather was scented like a
pot-pourri of spice and honey. She wanted to go
down on her knees and bury her face in it and might
have given in to the temptation if she hadn't noticed
in time someone resting against a boulder further
along the path.

As she drew nearer Ruth recognised who it
was—the girl who had vanished from the surgery
yesterday. She had discarded the coat which lay in
folds about her feet, and was sitting with her back
to the rock and a book on her lap, reading. Her
sleek dark hair, gleaming with a bluish tinge in the
sun, hung either side of her face. It was longer and
more luxuriant even than Ruth's and helped to
strengthen the idea that the girl looked like a
Madonna from a Renaissance painting. Her swollen
abdomen showed plainly beneath her loose cotton
dress, and yet she sat with a natural grace, her
beautiful face in profile, her chin resting on one
hand, and was so completely absorbed in her book
that she didn't hear Ruth approach.

When Ruth's shadow fell across her she looked
up and her recognition was instant. Then as if she
wanted to blank the memory out of her mind her
expression became impassive and she returned to
her reading. Ruth, feeling rebuffed, walked on, but
she had only gone a few paces when she changed
her mind and turned back. The girl obviously didn't
want to talk to her, but Ruth felt enough concern
to overlook that. In that brief moment before the
girl dropped her eyes, Ruth had seen in them an
unconscious cry for help. She couldn't ignore it.

The girl was still reading, or rather pretending to, for her eyes weren't moving. Ruth said, 'Excuse me, but didn't you come to the St Swithin's surgery yesterday?'

The girl sat there like a statue. Ruth was close enough to read the title of the book which was *Little Women*. That surprised her, it seemed such an old-fashioned book for a girl of that age to read. Presently the girl looked up. 'Yes, I was at the surgery,' she admitted. 'But I couldn't stay—I was late.'

She had a surprisingly light, almost childish voice which made Ruth wonder if she was younger than she looked, and that thought aroused in her some disquieting speculations.

'You don't mind if I keep you company for a minute?' she said chattily, seating herself on the heather. 'Do you live here in Jersey or are you on holiday?'

Again the other took her time answering. 'I'm visiting.' Her voice was cagey.

'I'm a visitor too, a working visitor you might say. Temporary nurse actually. It's my first visit to Jersey. What about you?' Ruth kept up the light informal tone.

But the girl wouldn't be drawn. She mumbled something Ruth didn't catch and turned to her book again.

Ruth hid her disappointment. She had a sudden gut-feeling that this girl desperately needed help, but was just as desperate not to let anybody know it. She was trembling, only slightly but sufficient for Ruth to feel the vibration, and her lips were clamped tightly together as if she was frightened of giving something away if she spoke again. It was no good—there was nothing Ruth felt she could do to break down the girl's reserve. With a sigh she got to her feet and as she did so the apple Pam had given her fell out of her pocket. It rolled along the ground and Ruth saw the girl's eyes following its movement, and something in her look made Ruth's heart lurch with pity. She recognised hunger when she saw it, and she was conscious at the same time of the girl's thinness, something she had failed to notice before because her mind her been intent on the pregnancy instead. The girl's arms were like sticks.

'When did you last eat?' Ruth asked abruptly.

Colour swept over the girl's face and up to her hair-line. She ducked her head and didn't answer. Once more Ruth went down on the ground beside her.

'Please do be sensible,' she pleaded. 'If you are too proud to accept help for yourself, think of your baby. It's due any minute now, isn't it? Don't turn away from me, I only want to help. You came to seek help yesterday, then lost your courage at the last minute, I guessed that. I don't know your history and I don't intend to pry but I just want you to know you can always find me at St Swithin House, so please don't hesitate to get in touch with me, any time.'

At last there were signs of a breakthrough. There was a noticeable easing of tension on the girl's part and she gave a long pent-up sigh as if releasing old fears. Ruth pushed her advantage home, and that was where she made her mistake.

'If there is anyone you would like me to contact for you—' she suggested, but got no further. She sensed the slight figure beside her go rigid, and the girl even grabbed her coat and draped it around her as if it were some form of defence. Purposefully she turned her head, but not quickly enough to hide the quivering of her mouth. Ruth put out her hand to touch her but the girl shrank away.

'Can't you leave me alone!' she said brokenly.

Ruth took the biscuits from her pocket and placed them next to the apple. 'I don't need these, I've decided to have lunch out,' she said softly, then walked quickly away.

She was determined not to look back, but where the path dropped suddenly she did take one last look round and saw that the girl was eating ravenously. Ruth felt choked.

It was downhill now all the way to St Swithin's Bay, and a pretty walk with late summer flowers, mostly mallow and wild chrysanthemums, edging the path, but Ruth hardly noticed. Normally she would have been savouring everything she saw and heard but now she couldn't get the pregnant girl out of her mind or forget her passionate words: 'Can't you leave me alone!' In her dream Matt had used the same expression and hearing those words again brought back the dream and the feeling of disquiet it had engendered. Ruth shivered and put on the anorak she had been carrying, yet the haze still shimmered over the sea and through a thin mist the sun shone warmly.

The path ended abruptly where the ruins of a wartime German blockhouse that had been built between the heath and the shore, a sinister reminder of an unhappy period in Jersey's history, barred her way. Ruth jumped down onto the beach, sinking into the soft fine sand. She took off her sandals and the sand trickled between her toes.

It was easier walking alongside the tide line, watching tiny crabs scuttling in and out of the seawrack. A dead star-fish had been left high and dry by the tide and a small boy was prodding at it with his spade. There were few holiday-makers on the beach; St Swithin's Bay didn't attract many visitors, there were no souvenir shops or ice-cream parlours, deck-chairs or boats for hire.

Ruth walked the length of the bay in the water, enjoying the feel of wavelets lapping against her legs. The sun and the water and the silk-like touch of the sea breeze on her cheeks acted like a tranquilliser, and disquieting thoughts of the girl and Matt faded from her mind. Ruth was just telling herself that it was time she turned back when someone from the beach hailed her.

It was hard to recognise whoever it was, as he was standing with his back to the sun—a tall fair-haired man in white trousers and a navy blue blazer. Ruth brushed her hair out of her eyes and squinted into the sun, then saw it was Tony Graver.

He came forward, grinning. 'Didn't I say so! You *are* a sea-nymph, and you've just emerged from Neptune's kingdom to call on me!'

'Complete with anorak and carrying my shoes,' Ruth quipped in return. She came out of the water and put on her sandals.

'Come along to the hotel and borrow a towel,' Tony suggested.

'My feet will soon dry in this sun.'

'Come and have a drink instead.' Tony wasn't easy to repel.

'I have to be back at the surgery soon,' answered Ruth reluctantly. A drink was just what she could do with, and Tony knew it.

'We'll make it a quickie then,' he said, taking her hand and pulling her laughingly in the direction of the Mirabelle.

A tray was brought out to them on the terrace. They sat under a striped umbrella at the far end overlooking the sea and surrounded by stone urns of deep blue hydrangeas. They were alone except for a seagull who perched on the verandah rail in the hope of tit-bits.

'Is this what you call a quickie?' queried Ruth, staring at the tall frosted glass that was placed in front of her. 'It looks more like a fruit salad.'

'It's a Pimms,' Tony informed her. 'Just the drink for a day like this.'

Once Ruth had got rid of the sprigs of mint and the tiny paper parasol that was poked into a cherry she was able to test Tony's assumption, and he was right. It was delicious even though the tumbler was so packed tight with fruit there was little room for liquid. 'I'm not going to waste these lovely bits of pineapple and kiwi fruit, but I shall need a spoon to get at them,' she said. 'Oh boy, what bliss. I didn't realise I was so peckish.'

'I'll get you a spoon.' Tony went off and returned with more than a spoon. He was also carrying a plate of sandwiches.

'I have a suspicion you haven't had your lunch yet,' he said as he seated himself, this time a little closer than necessary. 'Then be my guest, I haven't eaten either. Here you are, crab freshly caught this morning—just what the doctor ordered.' It was a slip of the tongue, doctor was the last word he had intended to use then for it brought just one name to both their minds. Their eyes met and though Tony was still smiling, it was a forced smile.

'Sorry,' he said awkwardly. 'I can tell by your expression that I've boobed. I was right, wasn't I—Owens did order you to keep away from me, that's why you didn't keep our date to go jogging this morning?'

Ruth was reluctant to answer such a direct

question. She put down her glass, the taste of the drink suddenly sour in her mouth. A few seconds before she had felt happy and relaxed and wonderfully at ease with this irrepressible man, but now she was gripped by such an irrational feeling of guilt that all enjoyment vanished.

Tony's mood had changed too. His grey eyes looked flinty and for the first time she noticed how thin his lips were. When he wasn't smiling he looked dour.

'Your silence is answer enough,' he said, trying to speak flippantly, but failing. 'My God, how that man can hate!'

'And all because of this hotel,' said Ruth spreading her hands in a gesture of disbelief.

'Is that what he told you!' Tony gave a short laugh. 'You didn't believe it, did you?'

'*He* didn't tell me, and yes I did,' Ruth admitted. 'Isn't that the reason for the feud then?'

Tony shrugged. He tipped his glass on one side swirling the dregs of his drink in an absent manner. 'I suppose the ill-feeling started when this place was built, yes. The Hackett Trust who own the Mirabelle thought there was a need of a good hotel in St Swithin's Bay. They approached old man Owens first and made him a good offer for St Swithin House. *That* would have made an ideal hotel—its own grounds, quiet, everything the Hackett Trust is renowned for—and as a private residence St Swithin House is nothing but a white elephant. It must cost a bomb to maintain, and as for having a surgery in such a way out place, whoever heard of such a thing. But of course the Trust came up against the DeBrice pride. The old house has been in the DeBrice family for generations, and though the family name was changed to Owens a hundred or more years ago, they're still carrying on as if they're lords of the manor.

'Do you know,' Tony leant forward, speaking slowly to emphasise each word, 'that what the Trust would have offered for that pile of ancient red granite would have set old Dr Owens up in a very lush modern house *and* left him enough over to build a modern surgery in the middle of the town, where it ought to be!'

Ruth considered this, trying to imagine how she would feel if she had DeBrice blood in her veins, and her sympathies were with the Owens. None of the patients she had seen so far had complained of the isolation of the surgery. One quite young woman had even said: 'I love coming here, it's got such an atmosphere. I always feel as if I'm stepping back into a kinder, more gracious world.'

Ruth looked reflectively at Tony. 'I think it would spoil St Swithin House to turn it into a hotel,' she said. 'It would lose its character. In no time at all there would be a swimming-pool and sauna baths, and the lovely old marble fireplaces would be ripped out and central heating put in—'

'Far more practical,' Tony interposed under his breath.

'And the french windows replaced by patio doors, and goodness knows what would happen to those old mullion windows,' Ruth looked and sounded so earnest that slowly Tony's sour expression changed to one more in keeping with his image. There was an enchantment about Ruth when she was serious that was reflected in her large eyes and the soft contours of her dimpled face, and which had a mellowing effect on him. He thought how attractive she looked with her velvety eyes and slightly flushed cheeks and the long rope of her golden hair hanging over one shoulder, and inwardly cursed the man who had this delightful creature captive under his roof.

It was this last thought that prompted him to say, 'Well then, let me tell you something. If the Owens had accepted the Trust's offer and moved into a modern house, Matt Owens' wife might still be alive!'

CHAPTER FIVE

IT took a little time for the significance of Tony's words to sink in. Ruth stared blankly at him.

'How can a house be the cause of anyone's death? Unless you mean—' Her eyes widened as a sudden thought struck her. 'Was there an accident in the house—did she fall or something? Oh, how dreadful.' All at once came a vision of a woman pitching headlong down the steep staircase, of a horrified child too shocked to scream for help. Was that why little Robbie had lost his powers of speech? Ruth waited anxiously for Tony's answer.

But he seemed reluctant to pursue the subject, even seemed to regret what he had said already. He still fidgeted with his empty glass.

'I don't know how she died,' he admitted finally, then added as an afterthought, 'Only Matt Owens knows the answer to that one.' He glanced up at Ruth from under his eyebrows. 'When I suggested that St Swithin House was the cause of Colette's death I didn't mean it literally. She hated that draughty old mausoleum, she would think up any excuse to get away from it. This hotel became a refuge for her. Matt Owens resented that, tried to stop her coming in the same way he warned you off me.'

Tony must have known Colette Owens well to be on first name terms, Ruth thought. Perhaps that was the real reason for the enmity between himself and

Matt. But something else he had said nagged at her even more.

'What did you mean when you said "only Matt Owens knows the answer to that one"?' she asked.

Again that long pause before Tony answered. 'I meant that Colette Owens suddenly disappeared from the scene—' He went on diffidently, 'She had a breakdown or something and Owens took her back to England for treatment, or so he said. She was never seen again in Jersey and a few months later we were told she had died in a nursing home. Funny thing is, nobody even saw the going of her.'

There was a hint of venom in his voice which didn't escape Ruth. She said heatedly, 'Are you suggesting there was something suspicious about her departure, that—that Dr Owens *disposed* of his wife in some way!'

Tony gave a thin smile. 'I wouldn't have used the words "disposed of" exactly, but I know Colette had become an embarrassment to him. He had just got himself this important post at the London University, but Colette refused to leave Jersey and go with him. That meant he was constantly travelling backwards and forwards and their relationship became strained. Colette didn't get on with her father-in-law either.'

Up until now Ruth had heard only good of the senior Dr Owens; Stephanie, Mrs Miller, Pam and all the patients held him in high esteem. She began to form an unfavourable opinion of Colette Owens.

'She didn't like St Swithin House and she didn't want to move to London. What *did* she want?' she asked somewhat impatiently.

'Just to go back to St Helier where she was born and lived until she met Matt Owens. St Swithin was too dull for her—she wanted the excitement of town life. She loved shops; she'd much rather go window shopping than gaze at the sea any day, though she enjoyed going down to the harbour and watching the boats coming and going. She loved movement and gaiety and something going on all the time. There's not much of that here!' Tony added dryly. 'And,' before Ruth could interrupt, 'I know just what you're about to say—that she could have got all that and more in London. But she was a Jersey-woman and had her roots here, she didn't want to move.'

'But good heavens, St Helier can't be more than half an hour by car. What was to stop her driving over every day if she wanted?'

'Because she didn't drive.'

Ruth's impatience was beginning to show. 'Then what was to stop her learning!'

'I didn't say she couldn't drive, I said she *didn't* drive. Matt wouldn't allow it. His car was too powerful for her and he made sure she didn't have one of her own, not that I blamed him. I let her try out mine once or twice and her driving was a bit erratic.'

Ruth felt Tony was hiding something behind that word erratic. Again that malicious look slid in and out of his eyes; she didn't like the way he told her just enough to raise doubts in her mind about both Matt and his wife, and wondered whether he was doing it purposely. The sound of a church clock striking two came from the hill overlooking the bay. Ruth jumped to her feet. 'Oh help, I should have been back at the surgery by now! And it's a twenty-minute hike, uphill half the way. Thanks for the drink—' she made to dash off but Tony grabbed her arm.

'It's less than ten minutes by road and my car's

already out. Here, take these with you, you can eat them on the way as you haven't had a bite yet.' He pushed the plate of sandwiches into her hands and laughed, and Ruth found herself responding. Tony was not the sort of man who would allow anyone to think ill of him for long—with the exception, Ruth reminded herself reluctantly, of Matt Owens.

They did the short drive to St Swithin House in less than ten minutes, which gave Ruth time to bolt two of the sandwiches. She didn't enjoy them, she was too worried about being late and also of being seen in the enemy's car, but Tony insisted. And she *was* seen, both by Mrs Miller and Matt, as Tony insisted on taking her to the door. Mrs Miller was picking roses from the circular flower-bed in the drive and Matt, hearing a car, looked out of the surgery window to see who it was.

The housekeeper greeted them with one of her tucked-in smiles, her eyes behind the thick glasses darting from one to the other of them with a pleased questioning look.

Ruth found she didn't have to make introductions, the housekeeper and the young manager already knew each other. She left them talking and ran into the house. There wasn't time to go up to the flat, or to do anything about her hair. She dumped her anorak on the hall chair, straightened her shirt and taking a deep breath walked resolutely towards the surgery.

Matt made no comment about her lateness nor remarked on her companion, which put Ruth at a disadvantage. She wanted the chance to explain that her meeting with Tony hadn't been planned, but as Matt didn't give her the opportunity she went about for the rest of the afternoon trying to stifle feelings of unnecessary guilt.

She tried to put Tony and his insinuations out of her mind, tried to obliterate them by concentrating on her work, but they kept erupting on the surface like irritations. What had he meant about Matt being the only one to know how Colette had died? What about Matt's father, he must have known too, a death wasn't something easily hushed up, unless . . . Was it the method of that death? Did something happen then that the Owens family didn't want publicised, and where did little Robbie come in all this? His mother had died in a London nursing home, the child had never been out of Jersey so it wasn't the shock of witnessing her death which had caused him to become mute as Ruth had first thought. That was followed by an idea that filled her with a chill apprehension. Perhaps Colette *did* die right here in St Swithin, and for some reason her death had been covered up. What else was it Tony had said? 'Nobody even saw the going of her.'

The implications of this were so horrific that Ruth immediately blocked them out of her mind. She couldn't believe Matt was a—no, she wouldn't even say the word to herself, but she couldn't entirely blot out the image of him as a haunted man.

The buzz as his light flashed on startled her out of her nightmarish thoughts. Her heart was still hammering away as she answered his summons, but when she saw him bent over his desk writing in his appointment diary she could have laughed aloud with relief.

He looked so normal, how could she have wronged him by believing such awful things about him. He looked up at her, was about to say something, then paused frowning, and his eyes showed a sudden concern. 'Are you feeling all right? You look rather pale.'

'I—I'm fine, thank you,' Ruth said with false conviction.

He seemed doubtful about that. 'I'd like to fix up for you to have a blood test sometime next week. I want to satisfy myself about your anaemia. It won't be in your own time, I'll run you over one morning. By the way, were you told about your free time? Weekends of course, unless there's an emergency, and one afternoon during the week.' His mood changed suddenly, his look of concern turned to one of disapproval. 'If you'd like to tell me which afternoon you'd like I'll make a note of it now, unless of course you want to discuss it with Mr Graver first.'

'Why should I have to discuss it with Tony Graver!' Ruth flared up, colour returning to her cheeks with a vengeance.

'Well, as you two hit it off so well I naturally assumed you'd want to spend any free time you had with him.' Ruth couldn't make up her mind whether Matt was deliberately trying to make her feel uncomfortable. If he was, he was succeeding.

'I have made no plans to see Mr Graver again,' she said coldly.

Matt gave her a look that brought her out in goose-pimples. 'I wish I could believe you. You told me you were skipping lunch in order to go for a walk—a stupid little lie, wasn't it? Especially when you must have planned to have lunch with Graver all along. And it was rather naïve of you to allow him to bring you back in his car. Did you think it would go unnoticed?'

Tears of frustration stung Ruth's eyes. 'I didn't lie—I *did* meet Tony accidentally!' she stormed. 'If you must know I was paddling at the time and wasn't even aware he was on the beach.' She didn't add that the only thing on her mind at that moment was the thought of the girl she had just left. She had been arguing with herself about the best way of finding out more about her when Tony had hailed her.

Matt brought her back to the present with a bleak, 'Please keep your voice down. You can be heard from the waiting-room.'

'It wouldn't matter, there's nobody there!' Ruth didn't mean to be impertinent, but that's how it sounded. Matt frowned, and in a more subdued manner she added, 'Mr Arley was the last patient.' As she spoke she drew her fingers across her eyes, wiping away the stubborn tears, and even that action seemed to annoy Matt for he winced and looked away. Ruth had no way of telling that even that simple gesture struck a chord in his memory too painful to bear.

'I have a message for you from Dr Raynor,' he said tonelessly. 'She said she won't be back tonight as she's going to a show and staying overnight in St Helier.'

Ruth returned to her own room trying not to attach any importance to this piece of news. It wasn't any of her business, but she was not surprised when shortly afterwards she heard the engine of Matt's car start up and then the sound of tyres on gravel, and assumed he had gone to meet Stephanie.

Ruth had a lonely meal in the kitchen of Stephanie's flat. By now she was really hungry and enjoyed the ham and salad she found in the fridge. There was a small portable television in the living-room but she didn't feel like watching it. Still, she had to keep her mind occupied somehow otherwise it would start churning out ideas she couldn't tolerate, so she decided to go and seek out Pamela's company.

She found her as usual in the kitchen, not working

for once, but curled up in an old-fashioned grand-father's chair with a magazine.

'I thought you'd be out on a lovely evening like this,' Ruth said to her as she squatted opposite on the bean bag which was one of the few concessions to modernity in this pleasant old kitchen.

Pam pulled a face. 'So did I, but my date let me down. He'd promised to take me to a disco in the town but he decided to play snooker with his pals instead. Wait till next time he asks me, he'll get a taste of my tongue pie!' Pam didn't look too disappointed. She said brightly, 'Like to try a bit of my chocolate cake.'

'I've just eaten, but I'd never say no to your cake.' Pam was a born cook, taking after her mother who had been a cook in domestic service.

There was some coffee to go with the cake, and the cake was delicious. Ruth chased the last crumb round her plate.

'Have some more,' said Pam.

'No, I couldn't, I'm just being greedy. Where's Mrs Miller?'

'Watching telly in her own sitting-room. She asked me to join her, but we never agree on what to watch. In any case, she goes to sleep halfway through and snores. There's a telly in the drawing-room if there's anything you want to see.'

'No thank you,' Ruth answered hastily, remembering the drawing-room with its beautiful painted ceiling and gilt-framed portraits of long dead DeBrices. It seemed a sacrilege to have a television set there. 'I'd rather sit here and talk to you if you don't mind.'

'Me mind talking! It's my favourite pastime. Sometimes I talk out of place, and that's how I lost my last job. But I was lucky enough to walk straight

into this job,' Pam went on cheerfully. 'I couldn't
have gone home, our Mum's got four on the dole
as it is. Me Dad, me two brothers and me. She relies
on the money I make in the summer to help her
through the winter. She's got a job herself, but only
part-time, cooking school dinners. I like it here and
the food's great. Mrs Miller is a good cook but she
lets me do most of it now. Dr Owens, that's the
older Dr Owens, the one who engaged me, he'd like
me to stay on permanently. He said I'm the best
little worker he's ever had. I don't mind work, I
thrive on it—but I couldn't stay on. Six months is
long enough to be away from home, and I'm getting
homesick.'

Pamela lapsed into a more sober mood. She began
to talk about the mining village she came from, the
unemployment and rundown streets of shops, closing
one after another because one-time customers could
no longer afford to patronize them. 'Jersey seemed
like paradise when I first came here,' she said. 'No
poverty, no dole queues, everybody looking so well
off. In the summer there are more jobs than people
to fill them, then they have to rely on immigrant
labour, Portuguese mostly. All the big hotels have
Portuguese waiters, and the best restaurants are
either French or Portuguese. You might even get
real cream there,' she added with a faint smile.

This reference to cream disturbed Ruth. The
following day was Saturday and she planned to go
to St Helier and find a shop where she could have
cream sent to her mother and to Sarah and to other
close friends. She had always done this when
holidaying in the West Country and she naturally
thought she could do it from Jersey. Now Pam had
raised doubts, and when Ruth enquired of her about
sending off cream the girl laughed sceptically.

'If you ever find a place that sells cream or sends it by post, let me know love, I'd like to hear about it.'

'But what about all the Jersey cows—all that delicious rich milk!'

'Yes, what about it—I've often asked myself that. Perhaps it's turned into dairy products like in Holland. Mind you, you don't see great herds of cows here like you do in England. Sometimes you see just one cow in a field and that's tethered like a horse.'

'Perhaps they are bulls,' Ruth suggested.

'Golly, I didn't think of that. Well, you wouldn't get much cream from a bull, would you!' Pam rose lazily to her feet. 'Time I took Mrs Miller in her supper tray. She always has two pieces of thin bread and butter and a cup of tea this time of night. Can I get you anything while I'm about it?'

Ruth declined. 'No thanks, I've eaten well. I think I'll go up and wash my hair. It takes ages to dry and I have the flat all to myself tonight as Dr Raynor is staying in St Helier so I shan't be in her way.'

'Dr Matt is staying out all night too,' Pam said in a significant tone of voice.

The buses to St Helier started their journey in the old town opposite the Mirabelle and then the next stage was at the beginning of the new parade of shops on the main road—a ten-minute walk from St Swithin House. But, Ruth argued with herself, if she took the long way round by the cliff path and caught the bus at the Mirabelle she might be lucky enough to meet the pregnant girl again. There was also the likelihood of running into Tony Graver but that was a risk she was willing to take. Ruth had spent a restless night with the girl on her mind (among other things) and knew there would be no peace for her until she had seen the girl once more and badgered her into accepting help.

It was a clear sparkling day with no sign of the previous day's mist. Warm enough, Ruth decided, to wear just a sun-top with her striped cotton skirt. She had braided her hair before going to bed, and now brushed out and hanging loose it rippled over her shoulders smelling faintly of the lemon verbena shampoo she had used.

Ruth was looking forward to this day out on her own browsing round the shops in St Helier; Pam had told her the market was a must too. The surgery didn't open on Saturdays and the Owens worked on a rota system with other GPs for the treatment of emergencies.

'And very nice too,' was Pam's comment, eyeing Ruth up and down as she came into the kitchen. 'I like your snazzy shopping bag—it looks great with your skirt.'

The bag was made from a piece of material left over from the skirt which Carole Richards had run up specially for Ruth to take with her to Jersey. It was a useful size bag with several compartments and gathered at the top into a large plastic ring that hung on Ruth's arm like a bangle. It carried Ruth's purse and wallet and, most important of all, her flexy friend; she was hoping to buy some souvenirs in St Helier.

'There's a young man waiting for you in the courtyard,' Pam told her without looking up from her task of boning a chicken.

Ruth's spirits sank, it could only be Tony—who else would wait out there? But when she went off to tell him that her plans were made for today and he was wasting his time waiting, the only person in sight was young Robbie, sitting patiently on an upturned half-barrel with his swimming trunks rolled in a towel under one arm. Ruth stared at him, puzzled at first, then suddenly remembered her conversation with him about going swimming. Her spirits plummeted even further, she couldn't bear to see disappointment cloud the toffee-brown eyes that were looking so trustingly at her.

'Oh Robbie dear,' she said, squatting down so that her face was on a level with his, 'I wasn't planning to go swimming this morning. Could we put it off until another day? I want to go to St Helier to do some shopping, but I don't know my way around there and I'm frightened of getting lost. Would you do me a favour and come with me to show me, and perhaps you also know some nice place where we could have lunch?'

Her ploy worked. Robbie didn't hesitate, his face lit up as he briefly nodded. He slipped down from the barrel and ran into the kitchen to leave his swimming things in safe-keeping. Ruth followed him.

'Do you think it'll be all right to take Robbie with me?' she said to Pam. 'Is Dr Owens around to ask?'

Pam gave her a meaningful look, she had to be tactful in front of Robbie. 'He's not back yet.'

'Then I'd better see Mrs Miller—'

'You'd better not, it would be more than your life is worth! She's closeted in her room doing the weekly household accounts. She takes ages over them. The poor old soul can't count for toffee and she's never mastered a pocket calculator.' The idea amused Pam.

'But I can't just take Robbie off for the day without telling anyone.'

'You've told me and I'll pass on the message when

Dr Matt comes in. Go on, it will do the little mite good to have some fun for a change.' Pam grinned at Robbie. 'Take him to Fort Regent—it's a leisure centre, all the kids love that. If there's trouble, I'll take the blame, my shoulders are broad enough!' Her grin deepened.

Ruth felt Robbie's eyes fixed on her with a look of burning intensity. He had taken in every word that had passed between the two girls and she knew that whatever the consequences she couldn't let him down now. While she hesitated he sidled up to her and slid one hand into hers and gave her a squeeze. That settled it. 'We'll be back about teatime,' she told Pam as they made for the front door. It was too far for Robbie to walk to the Mirabelle stop, so she would have to look out for the girl another day.

It was an enjoyable ride into St Helier, covering some of the ground over which Matt had brought her the day of her arrival. Robbie stared out of the window the whole way, but still clutching her hand and Ruth wondered if he was nervous of being separated, until it suddenly dawned on her that his concern was for *her*—he didn't want *her* to get lost, not after the way she had implied that she didn't know her way around. Ruth had a strong conviction then that if she could break through that off-putting wall of silence she would find an endearing and lovable child sheltering behind.

His likeness to his father was more evident in profile, the unnatural melancholy of his expression less so; he looked like a normal but solemn little boy on an outing, which he was. At one stop a bunch of noisy teenagers boarded the bus, speaking loudly to one another in German. Ruth placed them as students, flamboyantly dressed but well-behaved in spite of the upheaval they caused. One carried a flute and for the rest of the journey the passengers were entertained to some melodic haunting music. Nobody minded, the youth played well and gradually his companions fell silent as they grew more attentive.

The music had a marked affect on Robbie. He watched the flautist as if hypnotised, and the absorbed look on his face gave Ruth a sudden riveting idea. She wondered if it had ever occurred to anyone to let Robbie try to make sounds through music? If he could blow he could make a note, either with a harmonica or a tin whistle, better still a recorder. Ruth had learnt to play a recorder in junior school, but it was years since she had practised, and she doubted whether she could remember the fingering. But that didn't matter, she just wanted to see what Robbie would do with it. If it just aroused his interest it would be something. She couldn't wait now for the journey to end. As soon as they reached St Helier she was determined to find a music-shop, certain that she had found the key to unlock Robbie's tongue.

CHAPTER SIX

RUTH found St Helier much larger and busier than she had expected. She hadn't fully realised that as well as being the administrative capital and main shopping centre of Jersey, it was also a holiday resort and an important port.

The expansive harbour was the lifeline of the Island, the exit for the agricultural produce which was one of the mainstays of Jersey's economy and the entrance for the influx of visitors from England and France who disembarked in their thousands during the holiday period, for tourism was the second of Jersey's main industries. The marina built for the increasing number of private cruisers and yachts that visited the Island added to the colourful activity in the harbour, and from the many piers hydrofoils and speedy passenger craft took day passengers to the other Channel Islands as well as to France. Ruth, used to the long grey emptiness of the sea near her home town, was fascinated by the constant movement of shipping in and around St Helier.

Robbie had a look of careworn anxiety on his thin little face when they alighted at the bus terminus at the Weighbridge and Ruth guessed that his appointed task as her guide was now a weight on his mind; he found the crowds confusing. She bent down and whispered a word of encouragement. 'Don't worry, I think I can find my way around, and I can always ask the way if not. But just you keep tight hold of me in case I go wrong.' His eyes smiled in response, proud that he was still of some use, and Ruth put out of her mind any thoughts of personal shopping or sightseeing. Today she would give up to Robbie—there would always be another opportunity to please herself.

There was a French atmosphere about the town that showed not only in many of its street names, but also in some of the architecture. In other respects St Helier reminded Ruth of some of the more prosperous English resorts that still retained lingering Edwardian elegance. She thought it had something to do with style and an old time grace. But she was a romantic at heart, and everything she saw delighted her.

A maze of narrow streets led them to the main shopping precinct, and Ruth reluctantly averted her gaze from the shops that displayed wares from London and Paris. The prices were tempting too, as there was no VAT to bump up the expense, and she had to remind herself many times that she was looking for a musical instrument shop, not a perfumery or jewellers.

When they eventually found the right kind of music-shop, Robbie showed no interest in the transaction. He stood patiently by as Ruth made her purchase, not fidgeting as most children would have done for the elderly shopkeeper took his time. He didn't sell recorders every day of the week and he took a personal interest in displaying those he had in stock. He took Ruth and Robbie for brother and sister, and liked the girl's manner with the boy. He thought how well-behaved the boy was too, not like some who came into his shop, their fingers into everything. He watched the pair through the window as they walked away afterwards, the girl with her pretty golden hair swinging against her bare

shoulders and the child hanging on to her hand
looking up at her trustingly. The old man sighed.
They looked so young and vulnerable, he hoped the
world would treat them kindly, then he got annoyed
with himself for being a sentimental old fool, and
slammed the doors of the instrument cabinet shut
before going back to his office to make up his order
book.

The shopkeeper would have had quite a shock if
he could have seen into Ruth's mind at that moment.
She was troubled about Robbie. It was this detached
attitude of his that she found so unnerving, as if he
had insulated himself against normal emotions like
excitement and boredom and curiosity. In her
experience a quiet child was a sick child. There were
exceptions of course, and Robbie wasn't sick in the
physical sense—but oh, if he had only shown the
smallest interest in her purchase. He had not even
looked when the shopkeeper wrapped it up and
handed it over the counter, but had stared in that
disinterested way of his at the opposite wall.
Goodness knows what had been in his mind then.
Ruth began to have her doubts that the recorder
was the miracle worker she had hoped it might
be—more likely just another of her hare-brained
ideas that wasn't going to work.

But out in the streets again, caught up in the
cauldron of shoppers and sightseers, Ruth's optimism
soon revived. There was a gaiety and sense of vitality
in the air as if people being on holiday were hell-
bent on enjoying themselves and that was
infectious. Ruth entered into the mood, hastening her step so
as not to waste a single minute, and her silent
companion happily trotted along by her side.

They found their way to the famous Central
Market which had been described as one of the

finest in Europe and was majestically housed in a
late Victorian building of stone pillars and high-
domed glass ceiling. The centrepiece of the market
hall was an ornamental fountain, and here Ruth left
Robbie watching the goldfish in the surrounding
pool while she did her shopping. She had decided
not to have lunch in a café after all—it might pose
some difficulties when asking Robbie what he wanted
to eat. There was an abundance of vegetable stalls
in the market and Ruth had her pick of a delicious
variety of fruit; she also bought rolls and cheese and
two cans of Coca-Cola. Now all she needed was
somewhere suitable for a picnic.

It was by chance they discovered People's Park, a
large recreation area which included a children's
playground. They found a place to eat their lunch
with the tree-covered slopes of Westmount as a
backdrop and the sound of the playground within
earshot. Ruth glanced sideways at Robbie, expecting
him to show some reaction to the excited cries of
the children, but he went on munching his cheese
roll with the solemnity of expression she had come
to expect from him by now. Yet in a subdued
fashion he seemed happy enough, and Ruth got the
impression that just being in her company was
sufficient. He was a child who needed constant
reassurance and anybody he trusted could give him
that by just being there.

When they had finished eating Ruth took him off
to visit the playground, but taking him there was
one thing, getting him on a swing was another. It
took quite a bit of persuasion, but she managed it
in the end, and then she felt Robbie only obliged to
please her. She heard him give an audible sigh of
relief when it was time to leave. Having fun was
something Robbie would have to learn by degrees.

But the highlight of their day was the Fort Regent Entertainment Centre where one afternoon's visit could only ripple the surface of its many attractions. It was a town within a town, with shops, restaurants, theatres and the biggest fairground Ruth had ever visited. She tried, but couldn't entice Robbie on any of the rides with her; he seemed happy enough getting his enjoyment secondhand by watching others enjoying themselves. The giant snake slide held a fearful fascination for him and Ruth couldn't get him way from it.

At first he stared with apprehension as the children queued up to climb into its gaping mouth, but after hearing their shrieks of laughter coming from within the convoluted body, he soon became reassured and such a wistful look came into his toffee-brown eyes that Ruth's heart went out to him. She knew that he wanted to join the other children, but either timidity or something stronger—perhaps fear—held him back. The saddest thing of all was that he couldn't explain why.

In the tranquillity of the rose-garden Ruth took the opportunity of trying out the recorder on him. There was nobody around, and they found a quiet corner where the scent of the roses hung about them like a perfumed cloud and bees droned fitfully from blossom to blossom drunk on nectar. Ruth slipped off her high-heeled sandals. Her feet were aching after all the walking they had done, and she was amazed that Robbie showed no sign of flagging yet. He had the thin athletic carriage of his father, lean and wiry—perhaps there was more strength in his frail-looking body than she had given credit for. He sat with his knees supporting his chin and his arms wrapped round his legs, watching with his usual detachment as she took the recorder out of its wrapping.

Ruth was out of practice, her fingers felt all thumbs, but she was quite proud of her rendering of Three Blind Mice. She went on to Greensleeves, then Pop Goes the Weasel; she was halfway through Frère Jacques, but now so completely lost down memory lane that she was oblivious to her surroundings, when she was brought back to earth by a sharp tug on the recorder. Someone was trying to take it away from her! She looked up sharply, and there was Robbie shaking his head at her.

'What's the matter,' she asked surprised, 'didn't you like it?'

He gave another more emphatic shake of his head.

'Oh, you didn't.' Ruth felt suddenly deflated. 'But you enjoyed the flute on the bus, I could tell by the way you were listening.'

Robbie hunched his shoulders and spread out his hands. His gesture told Ruth as plainly as any words what he thought of the difference between her playing and that of the young German flautist. But there was something else too—there was a glint of mischief in the depths of his eyes that suddenly filled her with elation. He was mocking her!

She grabbed hold of him, rolled him over on the grass and tickled him in the ribs. 'You little imp—you're taking the mickey out of me. It wasn't as bad as all that, and if you think you can do better, show me!'

Ruth handed him the recorder, at the same holding her breath, wondering if it was going to be the battle of the swings all over again. But without any hesitation Robbie took the instrument, examined it closely all over then looked at her for guidance.

She showed him how to place it on his lips, how

to position his fingers, told him to blow softly. He was either too eager or too anxious because it didn't work for him. The only sound to issue from the recorder was a loud whoosh—he had blown too hard. Robbie stared at Ruth accusingly as if it were her fault.

'You're blowing too hard, dear,' she explained. 'Try again more gently—music has to be coaxed, not driven.'

He blew again—and again, but it was no use, he was still blowing too hard, and the only sound he made was like that of a despairing sigh. Then suddenly, in an angry reaction that took them both by surprise, he flung the recorder away as far as he could, then lay flat on the ground burying his face in his arms.

Ruth was jubilant. This was what she wanted to see, a good healthy fit of temper—at least it showed that underneath that mask of indifference there was a normal little boy struggling to get out. And she also felt she had made the first crack in his wall of silence—it wasn't breached yet by any means, but it began to show a weakness.

She pulled Robbie round to face her, hugging him tightly, and though he strained against her trying to break her hold, she was stronger than he was. His likeness to his father was marked—in the set of his mouth, the way his brows drew together across the bridge of his nose, and the sense of futility in his steady gaze.

Ruth found herself gritting her teeth in a frustration as fierce as his own had been. 'Scream, Robbie—shout—cry. Make any noise you like,' she begged him. 'Let all the pain come out, it will make you feel so much better. Oh Robbie, don't just accept—fight back—make an effort. Please darling, for my sake—for your daddy's sake.' But it was no use, she had lost him. His moment of awakening had come and gone, now he lay passive against her arm, his brief anger spent, his light brown eyes devoid of expression. He was safely back in his silent world of detachment. Ruth knew that for him the incident of the recorder had never taken place, he had already successfully blotted it out of his mind.

Perhaps, she told herself, his inability to make a sound wasn't psychological after all, perhaps it *was* due to some physical handicap. The experts, Matt and his father, could all be wrong—it was a harrowing thought which she hastily put to the back of her mind. She had come out today with the intention of enjoying herself and hopefully giving pleasure to Robbie at the same time. But all she had done so far was upset the poor kid with her amateurish attempt to make him behave more normally—she might even had undone any good she had so far achieved.

Ruth gave a deep sigh and at the sound of it he looked up and a trace of a smile lingered about the corners of his mouth. The look he gave her reassured her, and then when he slipped his hand into hers and squeezed it as if in comfort, the poignancy of the gesture brought tears to her eyes. They were back to square one and that was as good a base as any. 'Come along kiddo,' she said, assuming a false heartiness. 'Let's get ourselves an ice-cream.'

They took the cable car back to ground level for that. Swinging high above the town Ruth looked back at the ramparts of Fort Regent, the fortress built originally as a defence against Napoleon's forces, then when she turned to look seawards there was another fortress in sight, Elizabeth Castle rising from the tiny island L'Islet three quarters of a mile

out into the bay and constructed during the sixteenth
century to guard Jersey from her enemies. Two
fortresses, bulwarks of defence in times of war, one
now a pleasure centre and the other a museum.
Ruth had the fanciful idea that in a way they were
a modern version of how to beat swords into
ploughshares.

At the end of an enjoyable afternoon Ruth and
Robbie dawdled hand in hand along the Esplanade,
each happily licking a large ice-cream.

Neither looked as spruce as when they had alighted
from the bus at the Weighbridge. Robbie had an
orange moustache, a legacy from a recent glass of
orange-squash, and ice-cream had dripped through
his warm fingers onto the front of his shirt. Ruth
didn't look any tidier—the wind had played havoc
with her hair and the sun had dyed her back and
arms to the colour of a boiled lobster. Her clothes
were almost as crumpled as Robbie's, and because
her feet ached she had taken off her shoes and
stuffed them into her bag and was walking barefooted. She had tried to persuade Robbie to take his
sandals off also as a buckle was missing from one
and the strap was slapping up and down like a
dinghy in a mill race, but Robbie wouldn't part with
them, he didn't like the feel of the hot pavement
under his feet. And this was how they were strolling,
without an apparent care in the world, when they
walked slap into Matt Owens with an older man.

There was a moment of panic on Ruth's part
when she had a sudden vision of herself and Robbie
as seen through Matt's eyes. What would any of his
patients think if they had seen them and recognised
them, and for all Ruth knew they might have done.
An understanding smile on the face of Matt's
companion helped to restore her confidence, after

all who dressed formally on holiday? But she saw no sign of forbearance in Matt's expression, instead his hazel eyes sparkled with anger. Ruth shook the fringe out of her eyes, determined not to show any awkwardness.

It wasn't easy under the circumstances. Her ice-cream was now trickling through her fingers and running down to her elbow. Matt watched the flow with an expression of cold disdain. 'We've had a super day—we've seen and done about everything St Helier has to offer,' Ruth heard herself gabbling. Nervousness made her incoherent. 'We spent hours in Fort Regent and got so hot—that's why we're having an ice-cream, isn't it Robbie?' She appealed to the small boy who nodded shyly, looking at a point in the air midway between the two men. Like Ruth he seemed overcome by the unexpected encounter. Ruth made furtive glances around her to see if a litter-bin was in sight, all she wanted was to get rid of the wretched ice-cream. How could she exert her dignity holding on to a cone with its contents running down her arm? Any moment now Matt would introduce her to his companion, and both her hands were sticky.

'Alec, I don't think you've met Miss Richards yet, though I have mentioned her to you,' Matt was saying. 'Nurse, this is Dr Goodson. Dr Goodson is a colleague of mine at the hospital.'

Dr Goodson had a most practical way of putting Ruth at her ease. 'I think you want to get rid of this,' he said kindly. He took the ice-cream from her fingers and carried it over to a nearby litter-bin which Ruth's hurried glance had missed, dropped it in, took a handkerchief out of his breast-pocket and handed it to her, saying, 'After you, then we can shake hands without sticking to each other.'

Ruth could have kissed him out of sheer gratitude. He was short and rather rotund and old enough to be her father, but from that moment he was her knight in shining armour. When he shook hands with her he said, 'I believe I shall be seeing you on my department shortly?' And at Ruth's obvious surprise he explained, 'I'm in charge of the Path Lab and I understand from Matt that you've had some bother with anaemia and he wants you to come along for a blood test.' Dr Goodson chuckled. 'I must say, I've never seen a less likely candidate for anaemia than you are—you look positively blooming with good health. But you're going to regret burning your back and shoulders like that, young lady. Better get Matt to rub something on for you.' Ruth's face burned hotly at this lightly made remark. 'Seriously though,' Dr Goodson went on, 'I think it would be wise to come and have a check-up. I'll get my secretary to make an appointment and Matt can bring you along—perhaps towards the end of next week?'

Matt had taken a leaf out of Dr Goodson's book and was using his own handkerchief to clean Robbie up. The grimness of his expression had been replaced by one touching on tenderness as he administered to his small son. Ruth saw a look exchanged between them that was more profound than any words, making her realise once again the strength of the bond between the man and the boy. Matt nodded at his friend's enquiry. 'Yes, I can fit my time in to suit you.' As he straightened up, facing the full glare of the sun, the deep lines of unhappiness carved in his cheeks stood out prominently, and Ruth reflected that his night out with Stephanie hadn't helped to erase whatever memories there were that haunted him, but she got no consolation from that. Suffering in any form had a stultifying effect on her; for her own comfort she liked to have happy people around her, but could anything make this taciturn man happy again?

Matt said to Dr Goodson, 'I think I'd better run these two home—the sooner young Robbie is in the bath the better. Do you mind if we skip that drink after all.'

Before his colleague could answer Ruth blurted out, 'Oh no please, you mustn't think of it—really.' She made her appeal to Matt. 'It's only a short walk to the bus-stop from here and—and,' she had a sudden brainwave, 'Robbie was looking forward to the bus ride. He loves going on buses.'

Matt gave her a sharp look then smiled gravely at his son. 'Do you prefer buses, lad? You'd rather go home on the bus than in my car?'

Robbie nodded. Dr Goodson said, 'It's a treat for kids to go on a bus these days—it's an even greater treat for them to go on a train.'

Still Matt hesitated, and Ruth's heart thumped uncomfortably while he made his decision. For the past ten minutes she had been wishing for the ground to open and swallow her up. She wanted to get into a bath too, cool and scented if possible, and to change into fresh clothes and brush the tangles out of her hair. She didn't want Matt to go on seeing her as she looked now any longer than necessary.

Reluctantly he agreed. 'All right then, but I'll be home in time to see you off to bed Robbie. I missed it last night.' He didn't kiss his son, he wasn't a demonstrative man, but he gave the thin shoulder a gentle squeeze instead. Ruth felt that into that squeeze went all the love the man was capable of.

Dr Goodson shook hands with her once more.

'Well, I'll be seeing you, Miss Richards, or may I
call you Ruth?'

'Oh please do, it sounds so much more friendly.'
Ruth glanced sideways at Matt, hoping he had
overheard her answer for *he* never addressed her by
her first name. But he paid no attention, he was
looking out in the general direction of the Brittany
coast lost in a world of his own, and seemed startled
when Dr Goodson nudged him, bringing him back
to the present.

Ruth watched the two men as they went on their
way, Matt slowing down his long stride to keep pace
with his older companion. Dr Goodson's shoulders
were shaking as if he were enjoying a hearty laugh
and Ruth guessed she could be the reason. Matt
wasn't laughing, his disapproval clung to him like
an aura. He saw nothing amusing either in his son's
or his nurse's dishevelment.

That's the end of your image as a well-organised
person, Ruth told herself as she slipped into her
sandals. Every time Dr Matt thinks of you in future
he'll have an image of you walking barefooted along
the Esplanade with ice-cream running down your
arm. But she could also see the funny side of it and
she wasn't too worried. She had earned the father's
disapproval but she had gained the son's trust. That
mattered more to her at the moment.

It was fated that Ruth and Robbie were not to
catch the St Swithin bus after all. On their way to
the bus-stop a low-slung sports car with its hood
down drew level with them, and they were hailed by
the driver. Tony Graver didn't attempt to hide his
pleasure at meeting them unexpectedly like this.

'Hi there! You two look as if you've been painting
the town red!' He grinned familiarly, his eyes
sweeping Ruth from top to toe. Through Matt's eyes

Ruth had seen herself as an untidy slatternly creature; through Tony's she saw herself as a carefree gamine with a skin-tight sun-top that only just concealed her charms. She hastily pulled it up higher, returning Tony's salacious stare with a contemptuous one of her own, but he was too thick-skinned to mind. 'Can I give you a lift back to St Swithin?' he enquired.

'Thank you, but we're just about to catch the bus.'

He ignored the refusal implicit in Ruth's voice. 'There's a queue a mile long at the bus-stop!' he said airily. Even allowing for his exaggeration Ruth knew the buses would be crowded, shoppers and shop-assistants were starting their homeward trek. Her heart sank. 'Come along,' Tony urged. 'Don't be so stuffy, let me run you home.' He leant across and opened the car door. 'You'd like a ride in my car wouldn't you, young Robert?' Tony knew how to undermine Ruth's decision and he did it with another provocative grin.

Robbie looked at her with such pleading eyes, she had no alternative but to give in. How could a boy of Robbie's age resist a ride in a sports car! 'All right then,' she said ungraciously, 'but only as far as the bus-stop at St Swithin. We can walk from there.'

Tony didn't ask her why but there was a maddening look on his face as if he guessed the reason. He knew that Ruth didn't want to be seen arriving at the door of St Swithin House as had happened last time. And he was right—Ruth didn't want anyone to know Tony had given her and Robbie a lift home. If it got back to Matt's ears what would he think after his own offer to take her back had been refused?

They roared out of town, leaving the congested

streets behind them, Robbie sitting happily between Ruth and the driver. The wind clutched hold of his hair pulling it backwards across his head; with Ruth's it blew it across her face like a curtain and she parted it with both hands, laughing down at the boy beside her. Only Tony escaped the onslaught, his tightly-curled short blond hair was barely ruffled.

Ruth put her arm about Robbie's shoulders. 'Do you like going fast like this?' she asked.

He nodded without taking his eyes off the road in front. His thin little body felt tense with excitement—Robbie took his pleasures seriously. Suddenly a car behind hooted.

'And the same to you!' Tony retorted, at the same time pressing his foot a little harder on the accelerator. They spurted ahead but the powerful car behind quickly gained on them.

Tony looked in the off-side wing-mirror and grimaced. 'I think we're being followed,' he remarked with a touch of wry humour. 'Anyone we know?'

Something about his tone of voice put Ruth on her guard. She looked around hastily and recognised the Saab, and Matt himself glowering behind the wheel.

'Oh please slow down,' she begged. 'There'll be an accident if you go on with this mad race. Think of Robbie—'

'I'm thinking of myself too,' Tony retorted with surprising candour. 'I wouldn't stand an earthly against that car, but I don't particularly want to try. I hope your boss doesn't think I've kidnapped you against your will, he looks wild enough to believe anything.'

What could Matt believe? Ruth asked miserably of herself. That she had refused his offer of a lift home because she had previously made arrangements to meet Tony? That she had lied to him when she had said she was catching a bus for Robbie's sake? She felt sick at heart at the thought. Oh, what evil chance had caused him to change his mind and come after her!

By now Tony had begun to slow down. Again came a peremptory toot from behind but only to announce the fact that Matt was pulling out to overtake. The Saab swept past, its driver staring stiffly ahead, his profile a grim reminder to Ruth that there was a reckoning to come. Robbie recognised the car and clutched Ruth's arm and pointed.

'I know dear, that was your daddy,' she said lamely. 'He'll be home before we will.'

'You can say that again,' Tony muttered under his breath. 'The fool, going at that speed on a road like this!'

The encounter acted like a damper to their spirits. Tony fell silent, a mulish obstinate look about his mouth. Even little Robbie was affected by the sudden change of mood. He leant his head against Ruth's shoulder and began to suck his thumb.

CHAPTER SEVEN

IT wasn't Matt who was waiting with resentful eyes in the hall of St Swithin House, it was Mrs Miller. Deliberately ignoring Ruth, she rushed up to Robbie and lifted him up, kissing and cuddling him as if he had been missing for days.

'Oh, my poor little pet, what have they been doing to you!' she cried in tones of mournful suspicion. 'Just look what a state you are in and I put these clothes on clean this morning! You just come along with your Auntie Miller and get cleaned up, then I'll see about getting you something tasty for your supper. Something more suitable than orange-squash and ice-cream,' she added tartly, for there was evidence enough of that down Robbie's shirt front.

Ruth attempted to explain, to make her apologies, but the housekeeper gave her no chance, sweeping past her in such a manner as to show her displeasure. What she had said to Robbie had really been aimed at Ruth, a reminder to the interloper that Robbie was in her, Mrs Miller's care, and that Ruth had no right to horn in. It left Ruth with the conviction that she was back in the doghouse and she wondered how long it would be this time before she was released. She couldn't help being annoyed by the housekeeper's attitude, but at the same time felt sorry that they were at odds again.

Mrs Miller headed for the bathroom, her puffy face mottled with indignation, clasping Robbie's hand as if determined never to relinquish it again, and though he trotted along obediently he looked back once to give Ruth one of his sweet smiles. For Ruth that was sufficient recompense. Now to escape herself to a welcome bath.

But it wasn't to be. Matt appeared from a room to the right of the sweeping staircase, a room Ruth hadn't yet seen. He stood in the open doorway and said coldly, 'Would you come in here a moment?'

Ruth felt herself inwardly trembling with the effort not to show how nervous she was. Nerves mixed with an indignation that fate had put her into such a position. Good grief, all she had been trying to do was give a small boy a day's outing! And now look at the outcome—Matt, Tony Graver, Mrs Miller —each in their own way making her feel guilty. And she wasn't guilty of anything, that was the injustice of it.

Matt had prepared some carefully chosen words with which to scourge this impudent little makeshift who had made him look such a fool in front of Alec Goodson, and knowing Alec he would dine out on the story for weeks to come. And as for her blatant lies about taking the bus to please Robbie! At this point Matt was swept by a renewed ice-cold anger, but to his chagrin his anger began slowly to evaporate the more he looked into the face of the girl opposite. The defiant look in the large eyes staring back at him couldn't quite conceal a sense of apprehension, the full bottom lip quivered childishly and her whole stance was like that of a timid wild animal poised for flight. Matt suddenly hated the thought that he might appear frightening to her and just as suddenly her pretty troubled face was superseded by another that sprang unbidden from the depths of his memory.

An image of Colette's face became superimposed

on that of Ruth's—Colette's blue eyes staring at him
in that same half-defiant, half-fearful fashion. Colette
had been frightened of him—a fear that in the end
had been their undoing. Matt shut his eyes, wincing
at the memory, his expression taking on such a look
of lost hope that Ruth found her apprehension
draining away and a feeling of pity taking its place.

When he looked at her again his hazel eyes had
dulled over, the grim line of his mouth had relaxed
and it began to twitch. Not with amusement, he too
was having difficulty controlling his nerves.

'Look, I'll be honest with you,' he said after a
long pause. 'I had intended to bawl you out for
letting Robbie look such a mess. With any other
child it wouldn't have mattered. Personally, I don't
like to see kids looking as if they've just stepped out
of a bandbox, but that's how Mrs Miller has always
kept Robbie, and she's so good with him I don't
like to interfere. I get a lot of leg-pulling about it,
especially at the hospital—Immaculate Matt they
call me. Yes, that makes you smile, doesn't it. Now
perhaps you'll realise how I felt when I saw the two
of you, and why it gave Dr Goodson something to
hoot about.'

'I'm s-sorry,' Ruth stammered, realising she didn't
sound a bit sorry, she couldn't keep the laughter out
of her voice. 'But Robbie and I had such a super
day together—well, we just forgot about everything
else.'

'I know, I understand, and I'm grateful to you for
giving the boy a good time.' His eyes had warmed
to her, one of his rare smiles flickered on and off,
then he grew serious again. 'I just wish you hadn't
lied about that chap from the Mirabelle, that's all.'

Ruth felt her cheeks beginning to burn at the look
he gave her. It was more than reproach, it was a

look of disappointment that cut her to the heart. She didn't want him to think of her as a cheat. Quickly she explained what had happened, that Tony's sudden appearance had been as unexpected as his own.

'A day of surprises in fact,' he broke in with, and Ruth couldn't be sure or not if he was being sarcastic. 'I know I have no right to say this,' he went on, 'but I wish you wouldn't see that fellow. I don't like him.'

She could have retorted that the feeling was reciprocal but that wouldn't have done any good. She said instead, 'I don't plan to meet him—I'm not attracted to him in that way.'

'Which way?' His question came as swift as an arrow, catching her unawares and making her blush again.

'Well, you know—the way girls usually feel about men,' she answered awkwardly. Matt gave her a steady look.

'Do you often feel *that* way about men?' he asked as if intrigued.

Ruth wondered how he would react if she answered truthfully, 'Not often, only once so far—when I first saw you at St Helier Airport.' Oh, what scorn might she not release on her head ! She buttoned up her mouth into a provocative smile and said, 'That's my secret.'

'Fair enough.' Obviously Matt wasn't interested enough to probe further. 'By the way, this is my father's study and I use it when I'm home. If you want somewhere quiet to come to write letters or read, feel yourself free any time.'

It was not Ruth's idea of a man's study, it was more of a comfortable sitting-room with several chintz-covered easy-chairs and two sofas to match.

Like all the rooms in St Swithin House it had a high ceiling, this one covered with ornate plaster scroll work. There were two enormous gilt-framed mirrors, one over the high marble mantelpiece and the other on the wall facing the window. There were several small tables as well as a beautiful rosewood writing-bureau, and some delicate Chinese vases—one either end of the mantelpiece and others on the side-tables. Ruth felt sure that at one time this had been a woman's sitting-room, the elder Dr Owen's wife's perhaps? There were several photographs about, among them a wedding group. Ruth recognised Matt as the groom but only by his overall appearance: the face was that of a much younger, much happier man. His bride was simply dressed in a well-cut suit with just one adornment, an orchid pinned to the neck of the jacket. She was hatless and her fair hair shone in the sunlight, and she had the haunted look of one who was lost and bewildered and sad, the only unsmiling face in the group.

Ruth dragged her eyes away from the photograph to find Matt watching her, making her feel that she had been prying into something very private —making her want to run away from what she sensed as his intense remorse.

She did escape, leaving the silent man to his memories, and went up to Stephanie's room and wallowed in the long awaited scented bath. She changed into a backless cotton dress, for though the evening had turned cool she was now paying for her foolhardiness in catching the sun, for her back and shoulders were burning painfully and she couldn't bear anything against them. She had taken such care to ensure that Robbie wouldn't get sunburnt she had forgotten that she was far more vulnerable, having spent most of the summer under wraps as it were. Perhaps Stephanie might have something with which to treat sunburn, but Stephanie was still out and Ruth didn't know when to expect her.

It wasn't until an hour later when she came to turn out her bag that Ruth remembered the recorder, which she had retrieved from where Robbie had thrown it. Robbie would be in bed by now so she wouldn't be able to give it to him until the morning. Then she had a better idea. Why not leave it by his bedside? When he awoke he might be tempted to try it again, and perhaps, with luck, have success. Ruth was never one to disobey an impulse, and she knew where Robbie's room was. Pam had pointed it out to her when she had showed her over the rest of the house.

The door to Robbie's room was open and from the hallway Ruth could see him on his side, asleep. She crept in and laid the recorder carefully beside his pillow. Robbie looked angelic with his long dark gold lashes sweeping his flushed cheeks. His hair was still damp from the thorough wetting Mrs Miller had given it and it had curled into tiny red-gold tendrils on his forehead. Ruth had to restrain herself from kissing him.

She was about to tip-toe out again when Robbie stirred. He turned over on his back and she saw his eyes flickering beneath the thin eyelids and knew he was dreaming. Then suddenly he called out in his sleep, Ruth heard the one word—Mummy—but it was enough to freeze her to the spot. So Robbie *could* make sounds! There was *no* physical disability. She went nearer the bed, holding her breath, seeing that even in sleep the child was distressed as expressions of fear and panic crossed his face. Then he cried out again: 'Mummy—don't—don't. Mummy, don't jump!'

By now Ruth was thoroughly alarmed. Was this the result of sunstroke? She gently touched the boy's forehead and it burned under her hand. He was feverish and it was her fault—too much sun, too much excitement! She was too concerned to wonder at that moment about the full import of Robbie's words.

Then he grew quieter. He muttered something else which she couldn't quite catch, except for the one word, Daddy. The dream had worked itself out and he turned over on his side again and slipped off into deeper sleep. But his restlessness had dislodged the recorder and it had fallen on the floor. As Ruth replaced it on his pillow, Matt walked into the room.

If he was surprised at seeing her there, he didn't comment on it, he only said, 'I usually look in to say goodnight, but Robbie has beaten me to it tonight, and I promised to read to him.'

'It's my fault,' Ruth answered contritely. 'I have overtired him. He's had a bad dream. I heard him cry out.'

The look Matt flashed at her put her on her guard. 'Did you hear what he said?' he asked briskly.

Ruth wrestled with her conscience and decided to lie to save this man more heart-searching. 'No, not clearly, but enough to make me realise there's nothing wrong with Robbie's larynx after all. So my bright idea of the recorder was quite wasted.' He didn't follow her reasoning and frowned in puzzlement, until Ruth explained, then he gave her a thin smile.

'Not so wasted, I think Robbie will get a lot of pleasure out of it once he's mastered it. It was a kind thought, thank you—but I'm glad you have at last accepted that there is nothing physically the matter with my boy. I saw your doubts when I first explained to you.'

He was speaking about Robbie so easily now and without his former constraint that Ruth took courage to ask, 'But surely you're not going to accept that Robbie might be speechless for the rest of his life! Surely you can think of something to shock him into talking again?' Then she wished she hadn't spoken when she saw how Matt's expression had changed, how quickly her careless suggestion had rekindled the melancholy that was never far away.

He looked at her with a cold distant regard. 'I think my son has had enough shocks in his short life without anyone adding to them,' he said, and waited politely until she went away. Then she heard him close the bedroom door after her.

Ruth's period of unpopularity with Mrs Miller only lasted a few days. By Wednesday she was again in favour, the housekeeper coming into her room at lunchtime with something wrapped in a starched table napkin.

'I've just made a batch of scones,' she said, an uncertain little smile playing about her mouth. 'I know you like to take your lunch out-of-doors, and I thought these might come in useful. They're already buttered.'

Mrs Miller didn't find it easy to apologise, this was her way of saying she was sorry for her petty behaviour. Her grey eyes, magnified alarmingly by her glasses, were not completely guileless but Ruth was only too ready to meet her more than halfway.

'Oh, thank you,' she said, her relief at being on good terms again making her unnaturally effusive. 'I'll enjoy these—you just caught me, I was on my way out now.'

'I hope you're getting enough to eat up in that

flat.' Mrs Miller's voice implied she feared otherwise.
'You know you haven't been well, and you ought to
pamper yourself a little.'

'I'm fine and I'm in very capable hands. Dr
Raynor is keeping an eye on me.' That was a
mistake—the corners of Mrs Miller's small mouth
turned down sulkily. Ruth added hastily, 'You are
all being so kind to me, all of you making me feel
so much at home that I can't believe I've only been
here a week. It seems so much longer than that.'

Mrs Miller was all beams and smiles again as she
accompanied Ruth out through the kitchens and
into the courtyard. She went off to take in the
washing and Ruth followed the well-trodden path
she had made even in such a short time through the
pine woods and the wilderness garden to the greensward by the cliffs.

Monday and Tuesday had been busy days at the
surgery, but the work had eased off during the
morning and Matt, first checking he had no further
appointments until two that afternoon, had collected
his golf clubs for some practice shots on St Swithin's
course. He was an all-round sportsman Ruth had
discovered, which accounted for his lean athletic
build and overall look of fitness. He played cricket
as well as golf, swam well and had recently taken
up abseiling which he practised on the rocky cliffs
of the northern shores of the Island. Both Stephanie
and Robbie had gone with him on Sunday afternoon
to watch.

Ruth had spent Sunday wandering about the
cliffs, taking the path to St Swithin's Bay hoping to
see the pregnant girl again, but though there had
been a lot of people about there was no sign of the
girl. Ruth had wondered if she should take that as
a good sign, that it could have meant the girl had

gone back to her family. She spoke about her to Stephanie that evening.

Stephanie was in a happy mood, humming to herself as she unpacked the picnic bag she had taken for the trip to the north coast. Once she gave a quiet little chuckle to herself, obviously a legacy from a happy afternoon. The sun hadn't reddened her skin to the colour of boiled lobster as it had Ruth's but had brushed it with a patina of pale gold instead, and her eyes, borrowing the brilliant blue of her blouson jacket, glowed with a light of intense happiness. She looked like a woman in love.

Ruth stifled any lingering ideas of outdoing her and brought up the subject of the elusive girl. Either Stephanie didn't attach much importance to the affair or she was too involved with her private thoughts to let it bother her at the moment.

'There's nothing we can do, is there, Ruth?' she said, giving the younger girl a fleeting smile. 'Your offer to help the girl was turned down. What else could you do? I'll ask around and see if anybody knows anything about her. A girl of her age in her condition wouldn't go unnoticed for long, unless she's a visitor and already returned home. We can't keep tabs on everybody who comes to Jersey, you know. At present, I'm more concerned about you. How's that sunburn? Did the calamine lotion I got you work?'

Yes, the lotion had worked but not until Ruth had spent two uncomfortable nights feeling as if her skin was on fire. But now, idling along the cliff-top path, a light cotton jacket over her white shirt, the effects had worn off and today the sun was obscured by thin cloud. She walked as far as the boulder where she had last seen the pregnant teenager and sat there to eat her lunch. The only person to pass by was a middle-aged woman with a poodle on a lead, who, seeing that Ruth had something to eat, strained at his leash to get to her. The woman smilingly pulled him away, and the only company Ruth had from then on was a robin who was cheeky enough to come within reach when she threw crumbs.

There was still twenty minutes left before she was due back on duty, and Ruth took the letters she had received that morning from her pocket to read again. One from her mother and the other from Sarah, both in answer to those she had written to them.

Sarah's was brimming with apologies (she wrote as she spoke) for her part in the misunderstanding at the airport, but her contrition didn't prevent her from adding a hopeful postscript asking Ruth if she could bring her home a large bottle of her favourite perfume.

Carole Richards' letter too sounded like the writer—practical and businesslike and a little too perceptive for Ruth's comfort.

' . . . I'm glad to hear you are settling in so well and like it at St Swithin. You seem very fond of the little boy Robbie, and as you mention his father so often I wonder if the fondness has extended to him also. Beware of holiday romances, Ruth—all those flowers and pine trees and blue seas you describe so well seem to be having quite a heady effect on you. Don't do anything you'll regret later, my dear . . .'

Chance would be a fine thing, thought Ruth wistfully as she replaced the letter in its envelope. Matt only saw her as a helpmate in the surgery and perhaps as a companion for Robbie, besides which

Matt wasn't the sort of man to be disloyal to a steady relationship which he obviously had with Stephanie.

On her way back to St Swithin House Ruth kept her eyes peeled for a sight of the girl in the loose navy coat but without success. She had just decided with a certain amount of regret, for she was both curious and concerned about the girl, that it was unlikely she would ever see her again, when she caught a glimpse of her threading her way through a belt of trees that dipped down into a hollow. Ruth ran to catch her up.

'Hey there!' she called. 'I've been on the look-out for you. I wanted to see you. Wait, please—'

The girl couldn't hurry and didn't attempt to. She stood waiting for Ruth to catch up with her, looking shyly down at the ground.

'If we're going to keep meeting like this, we'd better know each other's names,' said Ruth cheerfully. 'Mine is Ruth . . .'

'I know. It's Nurse Richards, I enquired,' the girl responded.

'I see.' Ruth studied her thoughtfully. 'You wanted to see me again then?'

'I've been thinking over what you said.' The girl raised her head and her lustrous dark eyes searched Ruth's face as if seeking reassurance. Satisfied, they lost their cautious expression. 'My name is Florence.' This last remark sounded like a confession.

That's an unusual name for these days, Ruth told herself. This girl with her Madonna-like repose didn't look like a Florence.

'I hate it!' the girl burst out with a fervour Ruth had not suspected in her. 'The girls at school call me Flo, just to tease me. My second name is Anne, I'd rather you called me that.' She stopped, suddenly realising what her words had revealed, and a wary look came back to her eyes.

'Don't worry, I'd already guessed you were still a schoolgirl,' Ruth told her gently. 'How old are you, Anne?'

'I was sixteen yesterday.'

So that was why she had come out of hiding. She supposed that whoever was responsible for her condition was no longer in danger of the law. Was she protecting someone? Pity for this—this child swept over Ruth, and yet she didn't look a child. She was several inches taller than Ruth and her whole demeanour was that of someone maturer than her years. Ruth had the feeling that Anne had gone from infancy to adulthood without knowing what it was like to be a child, and she wondered what kind of parents she had who didn't know—or perhaps didn't care—what happened to their daughter.

She looked at her watch. 'I can spare you just ten minutes,' she said. 'But if you want me to help you, you must answer some questions.'

Ruth was late back for afternoon surgery and Matt could hardly contain his impatience. He was concerned for Mrs Mack who was waiting nervously to see him and felt Ruth's presence would help comfort her.

'Do you remember this patient?' he asked, giving Ruth his notes to read so that she could refresh her memory. 'It's the woman with the lump in her breast who was here last Thursday. You were very good with her, I remember. I've heard from the hospital and they have arranged to do a biopsy this coming Friday. Please show her in.'

There was a man sitting with Mrs Mack whom Ruth took to be her husband. He had a kind but careworn expression, or perhaps worry had given it a temporary gravity. He gave his wife a comforting squeeze as she rose to follow Ruth.

Matt had a certain way with him when dealing with nervous patients that put them at their ease. It took a little while to work with Mrs Mack as she was so tense. He told her about the hospital appointment for Friday, and that she was expected at Admissions at ten o'clock.

The colour faded from Mrs Mack's face, and she involuntarily gripped her bag with both hands. She looked fearful.

'I've heard such stories about lumps in the breast,' she said in a low unsteady voice, darting anxious glances at Ruth and then back to Matt. 'About women who go in for biopsies, and when they've come out of the anaesthetic they find that their breast has been removed. I don't want that to happen to me. I'd rather not have the biopsy if that's going to happen.'

Matt came round to the front of his desk, and perched on the edge. He reached out and touched Mrs Mack gently on her arm as if to reassure her. 'I promise you that isn't going to happen to you,' he said earnestly. 'The senior pathologist at the hospital, Dr Goodson, is an old friend of mine and he assures me that is not the practice at the hospital here. I've had a word with Mr Taylor, the surgeon in charge of your case, and he would like to see you and your husband if possible, before you go into the theatre, to explain to you just what the procedure entails. If you like I'll go over it with you.'

'Y-yes please . . .'

'Well, first of all a tiny section of the lump is removed and this is sent to the Path Lab. The histologist freezes the lump so that it is stable enough to cut into thin slices to be examined under the microscope. If there are any malignant cells this is reported at once to the surgeon, and then he will proceed with the mastectomy *only*, and I stress the word only, if the patient has already agreed to this before she was given the anaesthetic. Does that make you feel happier?'

'Oh yes, Doctor, thank you.' In her relief Mrs Mack started to cry, and Matt, looking up, caught Ruth's eye and such a heartfelt look passed between them that for one brief moment they were united in a bond of compassion.

Ruth accompanied Mrs Mack back to her husband. 'Could I make you a cup of tea?' she enquired, and Mrs Mack laughed. It was quite a cheerful laugh in spite of her tears. 'Tea, the panacea of all ills,' she said. 'But no thank you, my dear. It's very kind of you to offer, but I'd better get home, I'll have some arrangements to make now. And I think you'll be too busy to make tea anyway, the waiting-room looks nearly full.'

'I'll be glad to have some work to do, it was very quiet here this morning,' Ruth answered, helping Mrs Mack on with her coat. 'I'm coming up to the hospital myself at the end of the week to have a blood test, so I might see you there. In any case I wish you well. I'll be thinking of you.'

Mrs Mack didn't answer, but the look she gave Ruth expressed her appreciation for this little comfort. She walked out leaning on her husband's arm, seeming to draw strength from his nearness, and his head was inclined towards her as if protectively. Their closeness seemed to go deeper than mere physical touch.

At the end of the afternoon when the last patient had been dealt with and all the cases recorded, Ruth went into Matt's room and told him everything she knew about the girl, Anne. He listened carefully, his eyes narrowed in thought as Ruth repeated what she had found out, which wasn't a great deal. Anne still wasn't giving much away. She said she was staying with her grandmother but she wouldn't say who her grandmother was or where she lived. She hadn't any money and Ruth thought she had been living rough judging by her appearance. The only clothes she appeared to have were those she had on, and they weren't suitable for such unseasonal weather. As far as Ruth knew the girl had not attended an ante-natal clinic and seemed very vague about the date of the expected birth. What she wanted was somewhere to have her baby and Ruth had promised her she could have a bed at the surgery.

'What!' Matt sat bolt upright, his hazel eyes blazing with incredulity. 'You promised the girl she could come *here*? Were you out of your mind?'

'I would have promised anything to get her to co-operate,' Ruth retaliated, holding her ground though her heart was palpitating with apprehension. 'She's protecting somebody and that's keeping her from going to a doctor for help or going to a hospital. I only got her to promise to come here by saying there would be no questions asked, otherwise she wouldn't come anywhere near. She'd rather crawl off into the woods somewhere to have her baby, and I don't think she cares at the moment whether it lives or dies.'

Matt had got over his first shock. He regarded Ruth with a mixture of disbelief and annoyance, yet there was a flicker of amusement about his eyes too. 'Leaving the question of the girl aside for the moment,' he said, 'there's something I'd like to clear up about you first. Do you make a habit of going about disrupting other people's lives like this? You've only been here a week and in that time you've dressed me down for not doing anything about my son's speechlessness. You've upset Mrs Miller on two occasions, though I grant you that isn't difficult; you successfully organised your own sleeping arrangements, and now you've booked one of our wards for some unknown waif you've picked off the streets. May I ask whether you cause such mayhem in your hospital at home too?'

Ruth ignored the heavy sarcasm. She was hurt about the reference to her sleeping arrangements, considering that on that occasion she had been used as a pawn in a game that had started long before she came to St Swithin. 'You've omitted something else I've been guilty of,' she said meaningly, and instantly Matt's face assumed a closed expression and his eyes glittered ominously. He thought she was referring to Tony Graver, and she intended him to think that, but she said with all the innocence she could muster, 'I've also got Robbie to play the recorder. Did you hear him this morning, piping away in the kitchen? You must admit that was an achievement for me.'

He smiled grimly, in his turn ignoring her insolence. 'You're an unmitigated nuisance, but I must admit you have your uses. Now, about this girl. What plans have you made with her?'

'Nothing very definite. But I did make her promise to get in touch with me as soon as she feels the birth is imminent. I've given her the phone number of this surgery and also Dr Raynor's number, and I left her some change to pay for the phone call.'

'You've thought of everything,' Matt retorted drily. 'Well, it's on your own head. Don't ask me to play the part of the obstetrician when the time comes, I'm out of practice in that line. You'd better have a word with Stephanie, she'll help you.' He regarded her steadily for a moment or two, an obscure unreadable expression on his lean face. His hazel eyes looked strangely mocking. 'I hope this birth doesn't come off this Friday afternoon as I've booked for you to see Dr Goodson then. And afterwards—' he leaned nonchalantly in his chair, tipping it back so that it balanced on two legs only, lightly holding on to the desk with the tips of his fingers. 'Afterwards, I intend to take you on a little tour of Jersey and then find somewhere where we can dine. Does that meet with your approval or do you want to rearrange my plans?'

Ruth didn't even notice the sarcasm this time, she was too stunned, gazing at Matt with wide disbelieving eyes. He brought his chair back on the level and leaned forward, resting his elbows on the desk.

'I'm only trying to return the compliment,' he explained, amused by her amazement. 'You took my son out on the town, now I hope to do the same for you. And I promise I'll try not to bring you home looking as untidy and as grubby as Robbie did.'

Ruth smiled dutifully at this, but her mind was racing. Did Matt intend that they should dine tête-à-tête? It seemed like it—but what about Stephanie? A small frown puckered her smooth forehead and Matt said, 'You look uncertain. Have you got a prior date?'

Hotly she contested that assumption. 'You know very well I haven't dated anyone since I came to Jersey!'

'Well, now we can rectify that, can't we?' His manner was cool, slightly offhand, but the expression in his eyes was anything but indifferent. 'Your appointment at the hospital is for five—they shouldn't keep you long, and then the evening will be ours.'

Ruth walked back to her own room in a kind of dream. 'The evening will be ours.' She repeated the words to herself, wondering if she dare attach any significance to them and decided not. Matt was just doing what he considered the right thing—repaying her for her attention to Robbie. All the same her heart was singing as she went up to the flat to prepare supper.

CHAPTER EIGHT

IN the course of the next two days, Ruth found the opportunity to bring up the subject of the girl, Anne, and to discuss her case at length with Stephanie. Stephanie wasn't too happy about the girl having her baby at the surgery, and felt that the police should be informed. Ruth had wrestled with her conscience about this too, but she couldn't forget the promise she had made to Anne—that she would respect her confidence.

'After all,' Ruth pointed out to the still doubtful older woman, 'she can't have been notified as missing or we would have seen it in the papers or on the news—'

'Unless she has absconded from some home,' Stephanie mused, which conjecture guaranteed that Ruth spent a sleepless night, worrying.

But the following morning she awoke for the first time in days without Anne on her mind. The skies had been washed by rain during the early hours and now they sparkled like blue crystal. This was Friday—*her* day, and tonight Matt was taking her out on the town!

By three o'clock that afternoon all patients in the appointment book had been attended to. Matt called Ruth in to give her some accounts to be sent out, but as they weren't urgent he told her to hold them over until Monday. 'And now we can skive off,' he said, his voice as near to levity as Ruth had yet heard it. 'Stephanie will be back from her rounds soon, and she's promised to hold the fort for us for the rest of the afternoon. I shouldn't think there'll be much doing now. Would you like to go and get changed, and I'll get the car out.'

It was then that the phone rang. Matt answered it and Ruth, on her way out of the room, heard: 'Hallo. Oh, it's you John. Yes—yes, what's the verdict?' She turned, waiting, knowing it must concern Mrs Mack. John was Mr Taylor, the surgeon at the hospital.

Matt replaced the receiver with an expression of quiet satisfaction. 'That was from the hospital. It's good news concerning Mrs Mack—it was a benign tumour after all, and it has been successfully removed.'

Ruth sucked in her breath on a long sigh of relief. 'Oh, I'm so pleased—that's great news. Poor Mrs Mack, she fretted all those months for nothing. If only she had come for advice before, look at all the worry she would have spared herself.'

'It could have gone the other way,' Matt reminded her gravely.

'Oh, but it didn't, did it. Has she been told yet?'

'No, she hasn't fully recovered from the anaesthetic yet. Her husband knows, and he's with her. He wants to be the one to tell her.'

Now Ruth felt even more the joys of life as she hurried up to the flat to change. If the news had been different, if the tumour had proved malignant, could she have looked forward to her evening out with the same light-heartedness? Against all advice Ruth had always become emotionally involved with her patients—she suffered with them and she rejoiced with them. Tonight she could rejoice.

Deciding what to wear for the occasion caused her a minor headache. She couldn't turn up at the

Path Lab in anything too dressy, but if she went in something serviceable it might not be suitable for dining out later. She compromised by choosing a heavy silk pearl-grey skirt which had been a birthday present from her mother and as yet unworn, and to go with it a shell-pink jersey silk camisole-type blouse, just the right shade to compliment the slight flush on her cheeks.

What to do about her hair was another problem. At times like this she wished she wore it short, and though she was often tempted to have it cut, memories of her father always stopped her. He had been so proud of her hair, and it was no coincidence that the majority of the heroines in his books had waist-length golden hair and wide blue eyes.

Finally Ruth loosened it from its pins, brushed it out until it crackled with static electricity, then looped it at the nape of her neck into an abalone shell hair-slide. With a hot brush she fluffed up her fringe coaxing a slight curl into her dead straight hair. She was taking more trouble with her appearance than she had in months, and it was no good telling herself it was because this was the first time she had had a date in months. In her heart she knew she wanted Matt to be aware of her as a woman and not just as the temporary nurse he hadn't a very high opinion of. She didn't think she was cheating or being disloyal to Stephanie—Stephanie in some ways was a bit of an enigma.

For instance, later as she waved Matt and Ruth away, she showed no displeasure or annoyance at their going off together. Yet, when Ruth looked back for one last wave she surprised a look in the thoughtful eyes that she couldn't fathom. A look of envy perhaps, mingled with a certain amount of wistfulness?

With a sigh Ruth settled back in her seat and Matt, giving her a brief glance, remarked, 'You're looking very charming. Is that for Alec Goodson's benefit?'

'It is not!' Ruth answered through her teeth.

'I only supposed it because you've made quite a hit with him. He's staying behind to take a sample of your blood himself instead of leaving it to one of his minions. I'd better warn you though, he's a very happily married grandfather.'

If the rest of the evening is going to be like this I might just as well have worn sackcloth and ashes, Ruth told herself with a certain amount of resignation.

Matt didn't speak again until they had negotiated the busy main road and turned off into less congested byways. It was a longer way to the hospital but a more pleasant route. Then he said, 'There'll be an hour to spare before you're due at the lab. I want to call in at the orthopaedic ward to look up two of my father's old buddies who went in for minor operations. Would you like to wander around the town and we'll meet up later?'

'Could I wander around the hospital instead?' Ruth asked hopefully. She wanted to see how it compared with the large metropolitan hospital where she had done her training.

'Miss the old atmosphere, do you?' Matt gave her another glance, a faint smile quirking the corners of his lips. 'How long is it since you worked in a hospital?'

'Two months, but it seems longer.' Ruth looked back on the summer that had seemed to drift by in one wasted week after another.

'And what are your plans when your month here is up?'

That was a question Ruth had avoided asking herself for some days now. Once she had looked forward to the autumn and the chance of being back on the ward of St Catherine's as a staff nurse, now it seemed more of a threat than a long awaited dream. She had to face the realisation of a future outside Jersey—a future without Robbie and without Matt—and the thought cut deep into her heart. She couldn't answer Matt's question.

'I suppose you want to get yourself thoroughly fit before you make any plans,' Matt went on, unaware of her inner turmoil. 'Well, the first step will be negotiated this afternoon. If Alec Goodson gives you the all-clear we can build on that.'

It was comforting to hear him use the word we, but the comfort lasted only until she realised he was using the word in its broadest sense, that he was referring to the medical profession in general. She reminded herself that he too was only a bird of passage, that as soon as his father returned from his holiday, Matt would go back to St Jude's. Was that why Stephanie had looked so wistful? Ruth tried to cheer herself up by remembering that St Jude's was only separated from St Catherine's by the width of the Thames; but even that was a hollow cheerfulness, for distance or lack of it meant nothing to a man who was oblivious to love.

They reached the hospital as a church clock struck four. Matt parked in the space allocated for staff, locked the car and took Ruth through the main entrance.

'I tell you what you could do while you're here,' he suggested. 'Call in and see Mrs Sudbury. She's ready for discharge any time now—her visitors have fallen off this week and she's bored out of her mind. You'd be doing her a favour, besides which I'd like you to meet her.'

Ruth had to think twice before remembering who
Mrs Sudbury was—the nurse whose job she was
doing temporarily, of course! 'Oh yes, I'd like to,'
she said enthusiastically. 'I like to be able to put a
face to a name. I can tell her then what a mess I've
made of her books.'

That last had been added deliberately, Ruth hoping
to bait Matt into saying something like—'You've
coped very well, you've done a good job,'—but he
didn't oblige. He gave her a cool look out of his
hazel eyes which showed he had seen through her
ruse, and directed her to the gynaecology ward.

Because Mrs Sudbury was a nurse and a room
was available, she had been put in a small side-
ward. It had its advantages, it meant more privacy,
but it also meant long periods of loneliness, and
hearing the laughter and chit-chat coming from the
nearby main ward was at times particularly galling
for Sheila Sudbury, for she was a born gossip.

Except for the first three days of discomfort
following her hysterectomy she had enjoyed her
enforced idleness, but now it was beginning to pall
and she longed to be home. She looked up eagerly
when Ruth walked into her room and knew at once
who she was. Dr Raynor's description had been
accurate to the last detail, except that Ruth was
younger and prettier than expected. 'Don't tell me,'
she said. 'Miss Richards—or would you rather I
called you Nurse?'

'Neither, please—just Ruth. I didn't know I was
coming to see you or else I'd have bought you some
flowers or chocolates.'

'Look!' Mrs Sudbury gestured at the locker and
window-sill. Both were jam-packed with pot-plants
and vases of flowers, fruit, sweets, and get-well cards.

Ruth laughed. 'I see—it would have been coals to Newcastle. You must have a lot of friends.'

'A husband who spoils me and some very sweet patients. I've been overwhelmed by their kindness. How are you getting on? Please sit down and tell me everything. I'm just starving for news of the practice.'

Sheila Sudbury was an easy person to talk to as talking was her favourite pursuit, and one of the reasons she was so popular with patients was that she had the knack of putting them at their ease. She sat on the side of the bed in her dressing-gown hanging on to Ruth's every word, laughing uproariously over the mix-up at the airport and grimacing with sympathy at the recital of Mrs Miller's hurt feelings. The trouble with such people is that though they are easy to talk to they also unwittingly lay a trap for unwary tongues. Ruth found herself recounting things it would have been more diplomatic to have kept to herself. But she comforted herself with the thought that though Sheila Sudbury liked to chew people over it was not in any sense malicious. Malice was not part of her make-up.

Only tea interrupted their confab. 'I have some biscuits in my locker if you'd prefer them to the cake,' Mrs Sudbury said, and Ruth only just stopped herself in time from saying that she didn't want anything to eat as Matt was taking her out to dinner. That was something she very definitely didn't want to talk about, it was a pleasure too precious and too intimate to be shared.

Refreshed by her cup of tea Sheila Sudbury returned to what Ruth's Norfolk grandmother would have called a mardle, and on to a subject ever dear to her heart—little Robbie. She could remember in vivid detail the day he was born, the day of his christening, the day he took his first step, the mornings he spent with her while his mother was out, and—now her voice dropped and her expression saddened—the event that marked his illness and left him with a disability. 'He's not really mute, you know,' she told Ruth, her pale eyes watering. 'It's just that he's lost the power of speech.'

Ruth clasped her hands together, her palms growing moist. She felt on the brink of a revelation that was to have infinite importance for her.

'It's hard to believe he could ever speak,' she said with feeling.

'Oh my, he was a right little chatterbox. I bought him crayoning books to keep him quiet while I was looking after him otherwise I wouldn't have got any work done.' Sheila dabbed at her eyes. 'Of course, you've heard about his mother and her drink problem.' It was a statement of fact and not a question, and she was taken aback by Ruth's bewildered reaction. 'You *didn't* know!' she cried.

Ruth swallowed. Her mouth had suddenly gone dry. 'I—I hadn't a clue.'

'Good lord, then you're the only person in St Swithin who doesn't know about it—including the patients. Anyway, it's all old history by now . . .' Sheila's shoulders slumped dejectedly. 'Poor Dr Matt,' she said emotionally, not, Ruth noted 'Poor Mrs Owens.'

There was silence for a while after that. In the distance Ruth could hear the sound of a ship's hooter, it sounded as mournful as a lost soul in torment. Sheila dragged herself back from hurtful memories and looked at Ruth with moist eyes.

'I've said so much about the family I may as well tell you the rest,' she said. 'This isn't mere tittle-tattle, Ruth. I've been at St Swithin so long I feel like one of the family. Their joys are my joys, their sorrows mine too.' Her voice had lost its former exuberance and for the first time that afternoon she looked tired, and the effects of her recent operation began to show. She leaned back and rested against the high pillows, then recounted a story that held Ruth transfixed and for the first time gave her an insight into the pressures that had shaped the destiny of those at St Swithin House.

For a start Matt Owens had been Colette's second husband. Sheila Sudbury knew nothing about her first except that he had been a Frenchman, and Colette had divorced him. Drink had got a hold on her even before her marriage to Matt, though after they were married she had eased up on it for a while. Then when little Robbie was born she went into a state of deep depression and afterwards the drinking problem started all over again.

'And things got a lot worse after that beastly hotel was built—she didn't have to go so far for her drink then,' Sheila burst out with sudden vehemence.

'You mean the Mirabelle?' Ruth exclaimed. So that was the reason for the enmity between Tony Graver and Matt. Tony hadn't been entirely honest about it or his part in the trouble free from blame. No wonder Matt disliked and mistrusted him. Ruth felt angry with herself for having been misled by Tony's easy charm. 'So that's where Mrs Owens went off to when she left Robbie in your care?' she said, voicing her thoughts aloud.

Sheila shrugged. 'Some of the time, but she used to go off to St Helier too. I always knew when she was at the Mirabelle because she'd come home when the bar closed, but when she went to St Helier she'd stay all day and Dr Matt would have to go off and fetch her. I used to think that she hated St Swithin

House, that to her it was a kind of prison from which she was always trying to escape. Don't forget this was before Mrs Miller's time. There was help in the house, but always Portuguese girls and that posed a language problem. It wasn't a very happy place in those days, Ruth. Mrs Miller has her faults, but at least when she came she brought a certain stability. She helped to pull the family together after—'

'After what?' Ruth asked as the other's voice trailed off.

Sheila sighed. 'After Colette Owens died. I suppose you don't know about that either?'

Ruth recalled Tony's insinuations. 'I've heard rumours—'

'Oh yes, there are always rumours at such times.' Sheila stared unseeingly into the distance—or was it the past? Ruth wondered. 'One day when she had been drinking more heavily than usual, she attempted to commit suicide. She tried to throw herself over the cliff.' Sheila's lip curled. 'She timed it very nicely to coincide with the time Dr Matt was returning from the beach with little Robbie. He was there on the spot just at the right time to stop her jumping over. Little Robbie witnessed everything. He stood there with his mouth wide open, screaming yet making no sound. Dr Matt told me long after that it was uncanny and terrifying to watch that soundless scream.'

Memories of her dream came back to Ruth, of swirling mist and the figure of Matt trapped at the cliff edge wearing a look of utter despair. Had her dream been an after-image of something that had actually taken place? A feeling of chill foreboding tingled down her spine. 'Are you inferring that Mrs Owens had no intention of committing suicide—that it was just a cry for help?' she asked hesitantly.

The other woman squared her shoulders in a manner that showed her weariness. 'I don't know about a cry for help, she just made damn sure there was someone handy when she attempted to jump—that's what *I* think! Anyway, I didn't have any time for her, I was too busy with little Robbie on my hands. I nursed him for weeks—in one of the wards at St Swithin. If a child of three can have a nervous breakdown, then that's what he was suffering from, and I blame his mother. She never took any interest in him from the day he was born.' Sheila was bitter—it was hard to equate her now with the earlier bright-eyed gossip. 'While little Robbie was recovering I became ill myself. It was only flu but it kept me at home for weeks. When I returned to St Swithin House everything was different—it was the silence that hit me at first. Robbie had been a noisy little boy, constantly tearing up and down the passages, and shouting so that he could hear the echoes. Now he crept about like a little ghost unable to utter a sound. And Colette Owens could make a lot of noise too when she was in one of her drinking jags, screaming at everybody in sight. Now she was gone. Dr Matt had taken her to a nursing home in London for treatment but before anything could be done to help her she had a sudden heart-attack and died. You may think I'm hard for what I'm going to say, but I didn't regret her passing. She destroyed Dr Matt and she nearly destroyed that lovely little boy—I find it hard to forgive her. Then Mrs Miller came to take over the housekeeping, and Dr Matt went off to immerse himself in his new career at the London University, and Dr Raynor joined the practice and everything changed for the better. Except for poor Robbie.'

Sheila was spent, so much talking had wearied her; Ruth saw with a sudden rush of guilt that all colour had faded from her face.

'It's time you got right into bed and rested,' she said solicitously. 'I shouldn't have let you talk so much, I've worn you out.'

'Talking doesn't hurt me, my husband will vouch for that, it's the dredging up of old memories that's the trouble,' Sheila answered wanly. She readily allowed Ruth to assist her out of her dressing-gown and into bed. She took a sip of orange juice and her colour began to return. 'Don't look so worried,' she urged with an attempt at her former verve. 'I'll be as right as rain after a little nap. You must promise to visit me before you leave Jersey. Come and have tea with me one afternoon. We could have a lovely natter over the teacups.' She seemed reluctant to let Ruth go, but already her eyes were heavy with sleep. 'What a pity you can't stay on in Jersey.' Her voice was beginning to fade. 'I think we could have been good friends. In spite of the difference in our age we have a lot in common.'

Ruth gently disengaged her hand. 'You mean we're both nurses?'

'That too—but I was thinking principally about our feelings for little Robbie and his father.' Sheila's look of open candour was deceiving, underneath she was a very shrewd lady, and as Ruth walked away she wondered just how much she had inadvertently disclosed about the way she felt towards Matt.

By six-thirty the sun was a luminous bright ball giving an illusion of a gigantic orange just skimming the brim of the dancing sea. The sky had an opaque milky look, and a trail of tiny, tight-packed clouds were rimmed with gold. A mackerel sky, Matt told

Ruth, was a sign of bad weather to come.

Since leaving the hospital just a little more than an hour previously Ruth had hardly said a word. Matt hadn't seemed to notice her silence, or if he did, put it down to anxiety over her blood-test. Dr Goodson had promised the results as soon as possible; they could have waited for them, but Matt was anxious to get away, wanting to show Ruth as much of the Island as possible in daylight. Summer was passing and the evenings were drawing in rapidly.

He had driven her first to St Brelade with its long coastline and some of the prettiest beaches to be found in Jersey, and one of the most popular resorts as was evident from its fine hotels and amenities for the holiday-makers. They didn't stop to explore it on foot, Ruth had only a glimpse of the famous old stone church perched at the end of the wide bay and sharing its churchyard with the Fishermen's Chapel, which was even more steeped in history, then on to St Ouen's Bay to see La Corbière lighthouse. They arrived just as the sun was sinking towards the horizon and the lighthouse built onto a rocky promontory appeared as a silhouette against a sky flushed with saffron and rose. The tide was high and the sea was beating against the rocks. Matt explained that at low tide the lighthouse could be reached by foot, but sightseers had to be wary of incoming tides.

Ruth took it all in without saying much in return. Matt was a good companion once he got talking. He loved Jersey and seeing it again through Ruth's eyes seemed to enhance its attractions for him. Ruth was glad he didn't expect her to contribute to the conversation. Ever since leaving Sheila Sudbury her mind had dwelt on Matt's ill-fated marriage to Colette and the effects of the suicide attempt on little Robbie. Now Ruth understood the import of the words Robbie had muttered in his sleep; realised why Matt's hatred of the Mirabelle extended to its manager, and could understand and feel sympathetic towards the undercurrent of emotion that haunted St Swithin House.

From time to time she stole secret glances at Matt, the times when he was intent on his driving and wouldn't notice. Was it her imagination that he appeared more relaxed than when she had first met him? The sadness in his expression was less marked, the tenseness around his mouth lessened. This evening he looked, if not carefree (she couldn't imagine Matt ever looking carefree) then more at ease, not only with her but with himself. He looked younger too, though that might have something to do with his casual-looking outfit, sporty and smart at the same time. She was grateful to him for going to such pains to entertain her but she wouldn't allow herself to see anything more in it than his innate courtesy. He owed her a good turn and he was doing it, and being Matt, doing it thoroughly.

He was informative too—he explained why there was no scheme to send cream back to the mainland by post, and the explanation was so simple she wondered why she hadn't thought of it. The Jersey Milk Board did not manufacture clotted cream. Most of the milk collected by the Board went into the production of fresh milks, the rest into by-products. He told her something about the cows, those dainty deer-faced creatures Ruth had seen sometimes tethered singly, in tiny fields. They were so precious to the economy that they were not allowed off the Island. All Jersey cows were bred and raised in Jersey, those bulls who were shipped to the mainland as studs were not allowed back on

the Island in case they brought some infection back
with them.

'Am I boring you?' Matt asked suddenly. 'Are
you interested in knowing all this about Jersey?'

Ruth was interested in anything that interested
Matt. She was amazed with herself for ever thinking
his voice was clipped, cold and unfriendly. Tonight
its tone of camaraderie warmed her, and she leaned
her head against the back of her seat with her eyes
closed, happy to go on listening to him all evening.

After leaving La Corbière Matt drove inland
through unfrequented roads towards the east coast.
Daylight was fading fast and the eastern sky looked
ominous. 'I think our spell of fine weather is coming
to an end,' he prophesied. 'We've been lucky, we've
had unbroken sunshine for days, but the time of the
year is against us. We can expect the equinox gales
any time of the month now. When the weather is
very bad all shipping is cancelled between Jersey and
the other islands and Jersey and the French coast.'

Flights too? Ruth wondered, but that was too
much to hope for. Her time in Jersey was inexorably
coming to a close.

Matt's destination was the village of Gorey in the
parish of Grouville, an attractive little township
situated on the nearest headland to France. It was
still light enough to see in some detail the historic
stone castle that dominated the town, a grim
reminder of the days when Jersey was under attack
from its enemies. It reared up above the harbour
like a towering mountain of stone, bristling with
turrets and rounded by towers. Its last use as a
fortress was during the French Revolution, then it
fell into disrepair until in the early twentieth century
it was turned into a showpiece. During the Occupation, strengthened and updated by the Germans, it

once more became a fortress, this time in defence against the Allies. Ruth, listening to Matt's account of its history, found her thoughts suddenly diverted.

'Was your father affected by the Occupation?' she asked hesitantly, wondering if she was opening up old wounds.

'Not directly. He left Jersey in 1939 to go to London to study medicine, then war started and he joined the RAF. He was at a training camp in Canada when the Channel Islands were occupied. My grandparents suffered, naturally—not physically, but there was never enough food and there was always the worry of the enemy at the gates—literally in their case as German officers were billeted upon them.' Matt gave a short, somewhat self-conscious laugh. 'But that's all in the past—it happened a long time ago and there's no point in resurrecting old hatreds.' He twisted round in his seat so that he could look directly at her. 'You've been very quiet since we left the hospital. Not worried about the outcome of your blood test, are you?'

'I haven't given it another thought,' Ruth replied truthfully.

'Good, because I don't think you actually have anything to worry about. I can't see any traces of anaemia about you now. Let's see,' and taking her unawares he pulled down her lower eyelids, one after the other, and squinted at them closely. 'It's hard to tell in this half-light, but they look a good healthy blood colour to me. We'll know for sure tomorrow anyway. Come along, I've booked a table for seven o'clock.'

A short uphill walk from where Matt parked his car brought them to a restaurant which was quite plain and unassuming from its outward appearance.

Ruth would have walked past it without knowing it was a restaurant, but Matt was obviously familiar with it. The entrance was through a garden which now, as dusk was falling, was lit up by discreet concealed lighting. 'We can eat here or inside,' Matt said. 'I thought as it's so warm you might prefer to eat out-of-doors.'

It was romantic in the scented twilight, the tables were positioned within flowering arbours so that each one had the maximum of privacy. In the centre of the courtyard a fountain played in the middle of an ornamental pool, and for the rest of her life Ruth would remember that evening as one of star-studded skies, of the heady fragrance of jasmine and the sound of water trickling against stone—a combination that enhanced her already overcharged emotional condition, making her more susceptible than ever to the fascination of the man sitting opposite.

Matt ordered for them both. The restaurant was French, the waiters all Portuguese and few spoke English. They were quiet, efficient and very discreet, giving Ruth the disquieting idea that the restaurant—the courtyard at least—was a place for clandestine meetings. The restaurant proper was a blaze of light and from its open doors could be heard the strains of music. Ruth recognised snatches of Strauss and Lehar—all the ingredients in fact to make up a magical evening. But she would not surrender to the atmosphere entirely, reminding herself that she was but a temporary diversion in the complex life of this private man. How long would he remember her after she was gone? A day, a week, a month perhaps—whereas she would remember him to the end of her days. *That* was the difference between them.

The main course was served, a half a lobster in its shell lying on a bed of salad and topped with prawns in a cream sauce. Ruth was handed a thin steel instrument with which to dig out the flesh from the claws, and Matt showed her how to use it. The wine loosened her tongue and banished her last shreds of shyness. In the lamplight Matt's eyes glittered like jet, and they constantly flashed at her filling her with joy and despair in turn as she wrestled with her innate longing for him to love her. The lobster was delicious but Ruth couldn't finish it, she had eaten too much of the crisp French bread served with it. She refused a sweet, even an ice, but was glad of the coffee which she drank black, hoping it would steady her. She wasn't used to drink, and two glasses of wine could be her undoing.

Under the influence of the night and the good food and yes, perhaps the wine too, Matt had mellowed. Without any prompting from Ruth he began to tell her of his work at St Jude's and she was content to listen, knowing that her face was lost in the shadows and that she could adore him with her eyes in complete anonymity.

He told her first of his early years as his father's assistant, then his growing need for something more of a challenge in the medical field. He wanted to specialise but not as a clinician, there had always been a bit of a scientist in his make-up; as a small boy he had experimented with a chemistry set, had made slides to study under his father's microscope, and added to this was the conviction that to be able to prevent illness was of more use than merely to treat it.

'I decided to specialise as a pathologist and then to branch out into one of the many ramifications of pathology such as bacteriology,' he went on to explain. 'I took a year's sabbatical from the practice and studied at the London University to begin with, then spent my time winging backwards and forwards between Jersey and London until I had obtained my Membership of the Royal College of Pathologists. Three years ago I was offered the post of micro-biologist at St Jude's and I took it—' he paused, a growing restraint deepening his voice. Three years ago his wife had died, Ruth reminded herself. She locked her hands together beneath the table hoping the memory of that tragedy wouldn't come between Matt and herself now, just when he was most approachable. When he resumed speaking it was with a briskness that suggested time was running out.

'It's worked out pretty well. My father managed on his own for a time, Sheila Sudbury was invaluable to him during this period and Mrs Miller had joined the household and was running his home very smoothly, but my father was rising sixty and wanting to ease up a little, so he took on an assistant—the best day's work he ever did. Stephanie has been a godsend. Efficient, easy to get on with, a good companion, he was jolly lucky to have found her.' Each word extolling Stephanie's virtues was like a blow to Ruth. Not that she felt any rancour towards the other woman, she had long ago got over her initial reticence with Stephanie and now liked her exceedingly, but to hear how Matt's voice lightened when he mentioned her, how he spoke her name with such respect, filled Ruth with a sense of futility. This was proof, if she needed proof, of how much Stephanie meant to him. She gave a deep sigh which Matt heard. 'Come along,' he said kindly. 'It's been a long day for you, and you're tired. Time I got you back to St Swithin.'

He could be very gallant when he liked. He helped
her to her feet and helped her on with the knitted
jacket she had carried but not worn. But now the
evening had turned cool and a strong breeze was
rustling the tree-tops and Ruth was glad of its extra
warmth.

Gorey Castle, or Mount Orgueil as Matt
sometimes called it, stood out like a beacon against
the night sky, illuminated by powerful floodlights. It
was romanticised, turned by the effect of the lighting
into a brilliant scene of magic, its battlements
softened by patterns of light and shade, and by the
highlighted greenery carpeting the rocky escarp-
ments.

'It's beautiful—it's really beautiful,' cried Ruth
ecstatically, looking up at the monument with parted
lips. 'How romantic it looks at night lit up like
that—like a fairy castle.'

Matt had no eyes for the castle, only for her. The
floodlighting reflected on her face and enhanced the
soft contours of her cheeks, the sweet curves of her
mouth, the deep pools of her eyes. He felt his senses
stirring as old desires, long since dead, struggled into
life. A wave of sudden longing for this girl gave way
to a just as sudden illogical resentment that she
should have the power to arouse in him emotions
he thought he'd suppressed for ever. At the same
time, the thought that some callow young house-
officer might have prior claims to her filled him with
an impotent rage.

The drive home to St Swithin was difficult for
them both. Ruth sensed Matt's change of mood and
wondered what had brought it about; for his part
Matt found it impossible to get back into that state
of easy fellowship he had managed earlier. He
wouldn't admit even to himself the way this girl was

beginning to affect him or the feelings of guilt that
effect engendered, he only knew he had to fight a
mad impulse to take her in his arms and kiss that
pert pretty little face until his desires were satisfied.
He was so frightened of betraying these wayward
feelings that he retreated into silence, and Ruth,
sitting uncomfortably beside him, wondered with
growing despair why their happy evening together
had suddenly turned into a time of doubt and
dejection.

If she had known the truth behind its failure she
might have gone off to bed in a happier frame of
mind, certainly delighted that she could arouse such
strong feelings in Matt even if they were not backed
up by love, but Matt kept up his iron control to the
very end, leaving her abruptly at the door of St
Swithin House, saying he had to return to the
hospital.

Ruth knew that was just an excuse to escape from
her. He wasn't on the staff at the hospital and it was
too late for visiting. What had she done that he
should turn on her like this? She crept up the stairs
to the flat feeling shattered and in a way humiliated.
His silence put her in the wrong, made her feel
guilty, and yet she had a strong conviction that it
was *his* guilt that had come between them and she
wondered what that guilt could be. Later, she
thought she knew.

She was coming out of the bathroom after
showering ready for bed when the phone rang, and
she heard Stephanie answer it. The living-room door
was partly open and her voice carried.

'Yes, who's that?' Stephanie's voice rose in a
squeal of delight as she recognised the caller.
'*Matthew*—what a surprise! Oh darling, fancy you
ringing me! You what, you couldn't wait? Oh Matt,

you're just a big baby at heart, aren't you. Yes, of course I understand—don't give it another thought. You had no option, I realise that. Oh Matthew, I love you too, darling . . .'

Ruth crept away to her own little slip of a room. She had the answer to Matt's sudden change of mood now—it *was* guilt. He had taken Ruth out for the evening because he felt he owed it to her, perhaps even at Stephanie's suggestion, and he had enjoyed himself more than duty allowed and to ease his conscience had gone off to phone Stephanie from an outside call-box. It all worked out pat, but that was of little satisfaction to Ruth. She lay dry-eyed, beyond tears, watching the clouds scud past the waning moon. She had had her evening of enchantment and now she was paying the price.

CHAPTER NINE

MATT'S prediction of a change in the weather came true all too soon. Lying sleepless in bed that night Ruth heard the wind howling in from the sea, lashing the tree-tops and moaning down the chimney stacks. She had never liked the wind, it had always disturbed her, and now it seemed like some mocking spectre testing her nerves, demonstrating that the summer was over, that there was only the dying year to come. She indulged in the fancy that it was her own unhappiness taking wing and beating against a relentless fate.

But nothing seems so bad in daylight. By the following morning Ruth had pulled herself together enough to be able to face the facts.

If she had allowed her heart to get out of bounds it was entirely her own fault. Matt had never in any way led her to believe he had any interest in her other than as an employee. He had yet to call her by her Christian name—she was either Nurse or Miss Richards to him—yet on the strength of one outing together and because he had been so attentive, she had let herself hope that he was becoming interested in her. The phone call she had overheard had brought her back to earth with a jolt. Her mother had warned her that her imagination would get out of hand, and during that magic spell in the courtyard restaurant it had. She had seen more in the flash of his eyes than was evident, read more into his voice than he intended. It was her old

enemy, wishful thinking, taking control and now she
had to live with the consequences.

Ruth was never one to indulge in self-pity, and
nobody seeing her that morning would have guessed
at the aching heart beneath the crisp white blouse.
Certainly not Stephanie who was in such a buoyant
mood herself, she was hardly aware of what was
going on around her. Not Pam either who had spent
the previous evening at one of Jersey's highspots
and was suffering the consequences, nor Mrs Miller
who was coming to terms with the fact that she had
a rival in Ruth Richards where little Robbie was
concerned, but was trying to console herself with
the thought that Ruth wouldn't be with them for
much longer.

If it hadn't been for Robbie nobody would have
paid much attention to Ruth that morning, they all
seemed too wrapped up in their own affairs. That
included Matt who, entrenched in a mood of self-
detachment, nodded briefly to her without speaking
as they passed in the hall. He moved briskly as if
late for an appointment, and soon afterwards Ruth
heard the roar of an engine springing into life and
the crunch of tyres on gravel. Presently Stephanie
appeared, dressed to go out. She smiled at Robbie
who was trailing Ruth about like a shadow, clasping
his recorder. 'Have you made any plans for today?'
she enquired of Ruth.

Ruth hadn't given a thought as to what she was
going to do—the day yawned before her like a
chasm of emptiness. Robbie looked at her hopefully
and she said, 'No, I haven't made any plans, but I
expect Robbie and I will think up something to do,'
and was rewarded by a smile that lit up the whole
of his face.

'I don't know whether I shall be in for lunch or

not,' Stephanie mused. 'It all depends . . .' She shrugged happily, then went on her way humming under her breath. It depended on Matt of course, Ruth told herself. She said to Robbie, 'Do you know something, Rob—you and I, we're two orphans of the storm.' He took her literally and nodded solemnly, his eyes enormous. Outside the wind was whistling shrilly around the house.

It was a day for staying indoors. Mrs Miller lit a fire in the study and brought in some sewing to do, and little Robbie sat crossed-legged on the hearth-rug and played his recorder. After a while the continual tuneless piping began to fray Mrs Miller's nerves. She fidgeted with her glasses, then rubbed her forehead, and crossed and recrossed her ankles until Ruth, driven to pity for her, suggested that she took Robbie out for a walk.

Mrs Miller didn't care for that idea either, her expression turned sour and she sniffed. 'It's not very pleasant out, it's turned cold.' But she was too late with her protest, Robbie had already dashed away to fetch his coat.

'I'll only take Robbie as far as the cliffs and back. It'll give him an appetite for his lunch,' Ruth said, hoping that would mollify the housekeeper, but it didn't.

Mrs Miller was already in a huff over what she called Pam's hangover, and now little Robbie, her once constant companion, had transferred his favours to a newcomer, leaving her all on her own in this great empty house with not a soul to speak to! She felt very hard done by and wasn't going to put up with it! Leaving a scribbled message for Ruth on the kitchen table she went upstairs for her coat, collected her bag and her shopping basket and set off for the bus-stop. She battled against a wind that caught her breath and nearly blew her hat off and tried not to think of the cosy fire she had left behind. In other words Mrs Miller had cut off her nose to spite her face, but she was well practised in that art.

The temperature had dropped several degrees during the night, Ruth realised that as soon as she and Robbie left the shelter of the pine woods. Robbie was well wrapped up and Ruth thanked her lucky stars she had thought to pack her anorak. The wind came from the north-west, lashing the sea into a fury of white-capped waves that crashed relent- lessly against the cliffs. But the sky was still a brilliant blue, and when not obscured by cloud the sun was warm on their faces.

They walked hand in hand, Robbie still clutching his recorder. He wouldn't part with it now, it had become an obsession with him. Ruth wondered if he looked upon it as a kind of magic key that might unlock the door to his prison of silence, and that worried her. Robbie had too many psychological hang-ups already, she hoped she hadn't added another, but at least the recorder gave him pleasure, and with practice he might even learn to play a tune on it.

Then Robbie began to hang back, tugging at Ruth's hand as if he didn't want to go any further. She thought the wind was becoming too much for him until she noticed that his face had lost its colour and the sprinkling of freckles on his cheeks stood out like specks of sand against his white skin. He was also trembling.

'Robbie, you're cold,' she exclaimed, but his hand felt warm in hers—it wasn't cold but fear, she could tell that by his eyes. His gaze was fixed on the cliffs, and he was trying to pull her away, as if back to safety.

Could this be the spot where his mother had made her suicide attempt? Gently Ruth withdrew her hand from his grasp and going to the cliff edge, cautiously looked over. Yes, she had guessed correctly—immediately below was the cleft that she thought of as a bottomless pit. She stepped back, her heart pounding, heights always made her feel giddy and she didn't want the risk of a fall herself.

Robbie was wandering back to the house on his own and Ruth could tell by the way his shoulders quivered that he was crying. She ran after him and clasped him in her arms, feeling the sobs racking his thin little body as he clung to her. It was painful to have to *feel* the way he cried instead of being able to hear it. Ruth realised that by going to the cliff edge like that she had terrified the life out of him, no doubt reviving memories of the day that had changed his life.

She did not know how best to make it up to him, she could only cuddle him, stroke his head and wipe away the flowing tears. Slowly he came calmer, the sobbing ceased, and he leant with all his weight against her as if too tired to stand. Yet when she tried to pick him up he struggled. Ruth noticed that in all this time he still held on to his recorder—no crisis would separate him from that. She gave him another squeeze, then a swift kiss before he could resist. 'Let's go home and do some more practising,' she suggested, and he nodded.

Going back they had the wind behind them helping them on their way. Once the wind took hold of Ruth's pigtail and swung it across her face, and that amused Robbie. He had recovered from his shock and the colour was returning to his face. Children soon forget, they quickly get over things, Ruth told herself. But Robbie hadn't got over the greatest shock that had cost him his speech. That still lay buried in his subconscious.

The only sound in the garden as they climbed up to the house was the moaning of the wind in the pine trees. The magpies were silent, hiding from the onslaught on their roosts. The gale had scythed through the flower-beds leaving havoc in its wake, and Ruth saw that the delicate Jersey lilies had been flattened. She hoped Mrs Miller's prize geraniums had escaped the wind's fury; in their tubs in the sheltered courtyard they stood more chance than the plants in the open.

But the geraniums faded from her mind when she walked through the archway and saw who was waiting in the courtyard. It was the girl Anne, and by her expression Ruth could tell she was in pain.

Ruth ran to her. 'Is it the baby?' she asked urgently. 'Why didn't you phone as you promised!'

Anne gave a little moan. 'I—I couldn't, it all happened so suddenly.' Noticing Robbie she lowered her voice. 'I was on the cliffs when my waters broke—it was quicker to come straight here than to find a phone. I rang the bell, but nobody answered. I was getting desperate when I saw you coming—'

Ruth put her arm around her and helped her into the kitchen. Robbie trailed after them, his eyes wide and questioning, but when Ruth told him to run along and find Mrs Miller he trotted off without protest. With a sixth sense that young children and some animals seem to have in common he realised it would be better if he was out of the way. Ruth didn't know that Mrs Miller wasn't in the house, then she saw the note and took its message in at a glance. Pamela had gone to bed with nausea and sickness and she, Mrs Miller, was off to St Helier for the day.

Ruth fought back a sudden rise of panic as the realisation dawned that she was all on her own to deal with an imminent childbirth. Stephanie was out and there was no indication what time Matt would be home. In the circumstances Mrs Miller's or even Pam's help would have been invaluable. She tried not to let Anne guess at her state of mind as she helped her to one of the wards in the surgery, then undressed her and got her into the bed.

Though Anne's pains were becoming stronger and more frequent, the girl didn't utter a sound. At times her beautiful pale face was contorted in agony, but she had youth on her side and the suppleness of young bones to help her. Providing everything was normal, Ruth felt she might be able to manage, but if any complication should arise she decided to phone the hospital at once in spite of her promise to Anne. Lives came before promises.

During her training, Ruth had helped at confinements where Pethidine had been administered during labour, but she knew she wouldn't be allowed to give any form of analgesic unless under supervision. In any case, Anne seemed to be doing quite well without artificial aids.

The pains were getting stronger but Anne was using them sensibly, bearing down when they were at their height then relaxing when they lessened. It was almost as if she had attended classes on natural childbirth, and Ruth felt that all she had to do was stand by and give encouragement. Just her presence seemed sufficient, for Anne gripped Ruth's hand every time a fresh wave of pain convulsed her, turning crimson in the face as she strained. The baby came suddenly, there was just one short yelp from the young mother as the head appeared, then Anne fell back on her pillow exhausted. Her dark hair was plastered to her forehead, her eyes were hollow, but she was smiling as if in contentment. 'What is it, Nurse?' she asked feebly.

'A beautiful little girl. Another Anne!'

Ruth washed the baby and wrapped her in a clean towel as there were no baby-clothes available. Ruth had not exaggerated—the baby *was* beautiful, the colour of a peach and with a lot of downy black hair, and she was minute, like a doll.

'May I hold her?' came a small voice from the bed.

Ruth placed the child in the arms of her mother and watched as the girl's expression deepened in wonder. She touched the tiny fingers one by one, then bent and placed a soft kiss on the baby's forehead, her eyes bright with happy tears. She looked—Ruth struggled for the right phrase—like someone emerging from the shadows into sunshine.

Later, leaving Anne freshly washed and tidied and wearing a borrowed nightie, Ruth went off to make her a scratch lunch. Her pregnancy now ended, the girl looked thinner than ever, and there were obvious signs of malnutrition. At the moment she was too taken up with her baby daughter to care about material comforts, but Ruth knew it was vital to get some food inside her, especially if she was going to breast-feed the baby.

Ruth arrived at the kitchen at the same time as Pam. Poor Pam looked more in need of a doctor than Anne did. Her beautiful auburn hair was dull and straggly about her colourless face and her eyes looked washed-out and puffy.

'A-a-ah,' she groaned, flopping down at the table and supporting her head in her hands. 'Oh, heaven help me. I feel like death warmed up.'

'You shouldn't mix your drinks,' Ruth answered,

a little more sharply than justified. She was disappointed in Pam.

Pam gave her a reproachful look. 'I didn't mix my drinks, someone mixed them for me. I thought I was drinking a rum and Coke but some clever charlie tipped a Mickey Finn in it. I don't remember much after that, I passed out. I woke up this morning feeling awful. I did try to get up and do my work but the room kept spinning round. Mrs Miller tore me off a strip and now you're looking at me as if I've committed a cardinal sin. Oh—oh, I wish I was home. I want our Mam.'

She wasn't exactly crying, her voice sounded more like a dirge, but it was a cry for help and Ruth responded with all the warmth of her vulnerable heart. 'Oh Pam, I didn't mean to scold,' she said contritely. 'But I've had a hair-raising experience too.' She told the whey-faced girl about the new inmate of St Swithin House, and the news acted on Pam like a miracle cure. She staggered to her feet.

'Let me get to the coffee pot. Two cups of black coffee and I'll be as right as rain. A baby girl, you said? Oh, I love babies, I must go and see her. Why didn't you call me? I could have helped.'

Ruth refrained from saying that that might have meant two patients on her hands instead of one. But Pam amazed her by her powers of recovery; she was a good advocate for the saying 'where there's a will there's a way.' Though she tottered about the kitchen at first and left a trail of spillage in her wake, she soon had a dish of scrambled eggs, a plate of thinly cut bread and butter and a cup of weak tea set out on a tray. She wanted to carry the tray to the surgery herself, but Ruth firmly took it from her.

'Mrs Miller will be mad at having missed all this,' Pam confided in Ruth later when, Anne and her baby now sleeping peacefully, the others were taking the opportunity of having a belated lunch in the kitchen. 'She would have loved it, taking charge, giving orders. Mind you, I'm sorry I missed it myself, though I don't suppose I would have been much help.'

The wind had abated a little though it was still strong enough to rattle the windows and swirl up the dust in the courtyard, but it was cosy in the kitchen and they were all hungry. Even Pam had recovered her appetite by now, though she went without the bacon Robbie and Ruth were having with their eggs. She talked incessantly about the baby, and only Robbie's presence prevented her from pumping Ruth about Anne. She was eaten up with curiosity about the strange girl, and Ruth had to admit, though only to herself, that she was too. She hadn't even discovered Anne's second name yet.

Robbie ate his lunch like one absorbed but he was actually taking in every word that passed between the other two and guessed something of importance had happened. It was something pleasant, he could tell that by a sense of suppressed excitement that seemed to radiate about the room, and that reassured him. He didn't mind surprises as long as they were nice surprises. Mrs Miller's unexpected return just then turned out not to be such a nice surprise as it would once have been.

Mrs Miller had spent a frustrating morning in St Helier. It was too blustery and too busy, and where she had had lunch had been overcrowded and noisy. She had missed the bus back to St Swithin and rather than wait another hour had taken a taxi, so altogether her fit of pique had cost her dear.

Mrs Miller had looked forward to getting back to her comfortable chair by the fireside and to having a welcome cup of tea, hoping that Pam would have recovered sufficiently by now to make it for her. Hearing laughter coming from the kitchen she made straight for there, and much to her annoyance found Pam and the nurse and young Robbie still having their lunch at *three o'clock*! It looked very much as if her presence hadn't even been missed.

She was about to make some tart observation on this when Pam turned to her with a wide grin.

'You've missed the event of the year,' she said excitedly. 'We've had a baby at St Swithin House while you were out,' which remark only strengthened Mrs Miller's conviction that the girl had been drinking, until Ruth explained.

From then on Mrs Miller was a different woman. As Pam had predicted, she at once put herself in charge and Ruth wasn't sorry to hand over responsibility to someone else. A feeling of reaction was beginning to set in—a sense of weariness that was mental more than physical, but bringing rise to the old symptoms of anaemia. Mrs Miller noticed this and insisted she went off to rest. Her attitude towards Ruth had completely changed. Her old manner, which had veered between cosy friendliness one minute to resentment the next, had now given place to one of open admiration. She was deeply impressed by Ruth's handling of the morning's events and showed it.

Ruth took herself off to the bed in the second of the two wards; it would be nearer if she should be wanted than if she went up to the flat. She slipped off her shoes and lay down, not even bothering to remove the bed cover, and almost immediately floated off into a dreamless sleep. She awoke some hours later to an eerie silence and couldn't make out what it was at first until she realised that the wind

had stopped howling. The patch of sky she could
see through the window had darkened with heavy
cloud, giving the appearance of twilight. Ruth looked
at her watch and saw that it was just after six
o'clock! It would be twilight in reality very soon.

She swung into a sitting position and was putting
on her shoes when she heard the door open, and
thinking it was Pam sent to rouse her she said
without looking round, 'Yes, I'm just coming. You
shouldn't have let me sleep so long, you should have
called me.'

'I hadn't the heart to disturb you, you looked so
peaceful,' came the measured reply. Matt came
towards the bed, his hazel eyes glinting with mild
amusement. At the sight of him, Ruth had jumped
up from the bed in confusion. Her tee-shirt had
parted company from her jeans, and her hair was
falling loose from its braid. Sleep had flushed her
cheeks and deepened the brilliance of her blue eyes,
and Matt couldn't believe that this dishevelled little
creature had coped so efficiently with a childbirth.
Why, she looked little more than a child herself!

When he had arrived back at St Swithin House
that afternoon Matt had been met with the
astounding news of a new-born baby. He thought
Mrs Miller had taken leave of her senses and had
allowed her to lead him to the surgery to be introduced to mother and daughter in a state of disbelief.
Then Mrs Miller had told him of Ruth's part in the
affair, and he remembered then, Ruth telling him of
the young pregnant girl. He hadn't taken Ruth's
story very seriously at the time so it was quite a jolt
to him to come face to face with this strange young
woman occupying a ward in the surgery. He had
regarded her searchingly, wondering at the secrets
guarded by that pale composed face, but felt it was

too early yet to question her, besides which there were more important things to do first. He examined the baby, running his stethoscope lightly over the tiny chest, then checked to see if the cord had been cleanly cut. It had, and his admiration for Ruth, like Mrs Miller's, was growing all the time. He also did a quick superficial examination of the mother to satisfy himself all was well, and it was. Ruth and the girl deserved full marks for what they had achieved between them, and he told Anne so—then he went off to tell Ruth.

He stood at the side of the bed staring down at her sleeping form. She was lying flat on her back, her lips slightly parted, and strands of her hair trailed across the pillow exuding a faint aroma of lemons. Feelings that Matt had kept under control for years began to break through his iron reserve and he had an uncontrollable urge to take this helpless girl into his arms and kiss her back to wakefulness. But he still had sufficient will-power to stop himself giving in to such a weakness. Ruth had rekindled desires in him that he had long thought were dead—she meant more to him than he had thought possible, and he couldn't risk destroying her as he had once destroyed another.

He went quietly out of the room and shut the door behind him, and came face to face with Stephanie. 'Come along, I've got a surprise for you,' he said with false jauntiness, but Stephanie wasn't deceived. She had seen the look on his face when he had come out of the room and it filled her with sadness.

When next Matt went in to see if Ruth was awake he was in full control of his emotions. Now she stood awkwardly before him, surreptitiously pushing her tee-shirt back into her jeans and not making a very good job of it.

'Stop fidgeting,' said Matt, taking her arm not ungently and giving her a little shake. 'I've seen a few inches of bare flesh before, it's not going to shock me. I've come to tell you that you're dining with us tonight, and afterwards you and I will have to sit down and talk seriously about your patient.' He released her arm. 'Off with you and change—I know you won't feel comfortable until you do. And Ruth—' She stopped short at the door, her heart fluttering in her throat. It was the first time he had addressed her by her Christian name. She couldn't face him. She stood there with her back to him, feeling that even her back was vulnerable, that he could tell by the stiffness of her shoulders the importance his words had for her. 'Ruth,' he repeated gently, 'I just wanted to say—good girl—I'm proud of you.'

The discussion with him afterwards came as an anti-climax. Matt had put aside personal feelings and was at his most businesslike. Naturally he wanted to know all about Anne and was disappointed that Ruth could give him so few details.

'I've got to notify this birth,' he told her. 'I've got until Monday, and I'll give you until then to worm something out of that girl. If not, I'll have to inform the police.'

Ruth knew he didn't want to do that, he had a morbid dread of publicity of any kind, and she could imagine how the local papers would go to town with such a story. It was the old DeBrice pride she supposed, recoiling from anything that smacked of sensationalism. But she had no luck with Anne. To every question she was asked she simply said, 'I don't remember'. Ruth began to believe her. She remembered a case once where a woman had gone

completely deaf during a difficult labour, but Anne
had had an easy time, so that couldn't be the answer.
Could she be so guileless, lying there with her saint-
like expression, making no demands, asking no
favours. She was the easiest patient Ruth had ever
nursed.

Mrs Miller, perhaps, was enjoying the event more
than anybody. She was at her best with children and
to her Anne was still a child; she fussed over her
and the baby equally. From some corner of the attic
she had unearthed the carry-cot that had once
belonged to Robbie, and also some of his baby
things she had discovered stored away between sheets
of tissue paper when she first came to St Swithin
House. Perhaps by Sheila Sudbury, she suggested
now to Ruth.

Mrs Miller's attitude towards Anne surprised
Ruth, who had expected her to disapprove strongly
of the fact of a schoolgirl giving birth. Nothing of
the kind. Whatever she thought privately about the
affair she kept to herself, outwardly she was all
warmth and kindness and Ruth formed the opinion
that the young brought out the best in Mrs Miller's
character. She seemed to like children more than she
liked adults, she was certainly more at home with
them.

Monday morning brought Ruth the breakthrough
with Anne that she had been striving for and it came
about without any planning. About ten o'clock a
sheaf of large shaggy white chrysanthemums was
delivered to the house, and Ruth, who happened to
be near the door when the florist rang, took them
in. Naturally she thought someone had sent them
for Anne. Her mind hadn't gone further than that
when she saw that the card was addressed to herself.

With mixed feelings she turned the card over,

hoping Tony wasn't surfacing into her life again,
but her fears were groundless. The flowers were from
Mrs Mack, the patient who had gone into hospital
for a biopsy.

Dear Nurse, she had written,
 Just a small way to show my appreciation
for your kindness and care of me. I've been a
very foolish woman and put myself and my
dear husband through a lot of unnecessary
worrying, but I am so happy now I feel a
different person.

          With grateful thanks and best wishes,

          Iris Mack

Tears welled into Ruth's eyes. She was easily
touched by kindness and this was more than kind
of Mrs Mack, after all Ruth had just been doing her
job. The flowers were beautiful—each one a hot-
house bloom. On an impulse Ruth decided to take
them to Anne. Mrs Miller had picked some flowers
from the garden but the gales hadn't left many
undamaged, and she had only been able to find
enough to fill one small vase.
 When Anne saw the chrysanthemums her face
flushed with pleasure. 'For me?' she asked unstea-
dily.
 'From me to you,' Ruth said brightly. She saw
that Anne was still poring over the dictionary of
first names that Pam had lent her. The baby was as
yet unnamed and everybody called her Little
Anne—Little Orphan Annie, quipped Pam in the
privacy of the kitchen when Mrs Miller wasn't
around.

Ruth went over and sat on the bed. 'This room looks very bare without flowers and cards, not a bit like a maternity ward,' she said wistfully. 'Most of the mothers I nursed at my hospital planned to keep all their greeting cards to stick in a baby album.' Ruth looked earnestly at the girl who dropped her eyes, suddenly on the defensive. 'Anne, do you realise you are depriving your child of her birthright? Somewhere she has a father and grandparents and other relatives, you can't keep her a secret indefinitely and they have a right to know about her, she is part of their flesh too. I know you're only sixteen, but you're no longer a child, you are a woman and a parent and that carries certain responsibilities. That little baby over there owes you nothing, but you owe her a future and security and the love and care of a family. If you love her you'll stop thinking of yourself, you'll stop thinking of whoever it is you're trying to shield—you'll think only of her and what is best for her. That's the true test of mother love.'

Ruth had rarely spoken with such passion. Her words came straight from her heart, unrehearsed and unplanned. Perhaps because of that they succeeded in getting through.

Tears had gathered in Anne's eyes and slipped unheeded down her cheeks. She looked across at the cot where the only visible signs of the wakeful occupant were two tiny fists punching the air, then she looked at Ruth and gave her a tremulous smile. 'Would you please get in touch with my mother and father?' she asked softly.

Half an hour later Ruth knocked on Matt's door and went in. He looked up impatiently, his brow contracted in a frown. The last he had seen of his nurse was when she had helped a frail old lady to

the door and then out to a waiting car; Ruth should
have returned immediately but she was nearly three
quarters of an hour late and he suspected she had
been doing a spot of baby-worship. Worry about
the mysterious young mother and the way she was
wrecking the daily routine wasn't doing anything for
Matt's temper. 'Where have you been?' he demanded
brusquely. 'Don't you realise there are other legiti-
mate patients waiting out there!'

Ruth only smiled. Coming straight from Anne's
pent-up confidences, gratified and in a small way
triumphant at her success, she could afford to look
at Matt with a certain complacency. She place a slip
of paper before him.

'That's the phone number of Anne's parents,' she
said, rejoicing at the look of relief that came over
him. 'She asked if you would please get in touch
with them for her.'

CHAPTER TEN

THE storm that had blown itself out in less than twenty-four hours marked the end of the late summer heatwave. Now autumn was just around the corner and the wind had a keen edge to it.

Ruth walked along the cliff path, her hands thrust deep in the pockets of her padded anorak, trying not to dwell on the fact that in a week's time she would be back in Norfolk, and a week after that back at St Catherine's as a staff nurse on children's surgical. Her mother had forwarded a letter from the hospital offering Ruth the post and she had written and accepted just after Anne's parents flew in to Jersey.

Ruth had gone with Matt to meet them at the airport. He had phoned them on the Monday after hearing Anne's story; Ruth had given him the gist of what Anne had confided in her but she couldn't reproduce the anguish and the guilt and the sense of failure that had overcharged the girl's voice.

It wasn't an uncommon story—a girl born to parents, both in their forties, who had carved out successful careers for themselves in the academic world and found the advent of an unplanned child something of an embarrassment. She had been denied nothing except their time and attention, and sometimes she thought, their love—she got that from the temporary nannies who drifted in and out of her life. The one steady relationship which was Anne's anchor in life was that with her grandmother, and she had spent all her school holidays with her here in Jersey, for that was when her parents went travelling, either on lecture tours or taking parties of students on educational holidays to other countries.

But the previous Easter Mrs Marshall had suffered a severe stroke and died shortly afterwards, and her house which had been left to her only son was temporarily boarded up until a decision had been made whether to sell it or use it as a holiday home.

By this time Anne knew she was pregnant and now with the loss of her grandmother she had nobody to turn to. She was at a boarding-school in Hampshire and she wrote and told her parents that she had had an invitation to spend the whole of the summer holidays with the family of a school friend in Scotland.

This news suited the Marshalls as they had planned to spend the long vacation on some research work in Greece and had wondered what to do with their daughter. Adèle Marshall had dutifully sent off a letter of thanks to the Scottish family in Perth who had so kindly offered their hospitality to Anne for the summer.

The letter had mystified Mrs MacGregor until she vaguely recalled the Marshalls and their reputation for being the prototype absent-minded professors, and thinking they had mixed her up with someone else, she dismissed it from her mind.

The school uniform with its loose overall-type dresses had helped to disguise Anne's thickening figure. Then in the middle of July when school broke up she withdrew all her savings from the post office and sailed to Jersey. She hadn't thought further ahead than that—she only knew she had to get back to the only place she thought of as home and find shelter there—like a wounded animal to its lair.

She had a key to a side door of her grandmother's house and had let herself in under cover of darkness in case anybody saw her, but there was very little danger of that. The house was situated near the cliffs in the opposite direction to the bay and shrouded by trees, and was some distance from other residences, but Anne had now reached the state where she believed everybody was spying on her and went out of her way to avoid being seen.

The furniture was under dust covers and the beds had been stripped, so she slept on cushions on the floor. Water and electricity had been cut off and the pantry was bare, but down in the cellar she found some withered apples and pears left over from the previous autumn, and with the remainder of her money to spend on food had lived adequately for the first month. However, the day Ruth had come across her reading one of her grandmother's books she hadn't eaten for twenty-four hours.

'What did you do after that?' Ruth asked, her heart torn with anguish by this girl's story.

'I—I sold something,' came the reluctant reply.

There were gaps in the girl's story—not once did she mention the father, and when Ruth tried to bring his name into the conversation she was met with a passive resistance more potent than downright defiance. It didn't matter at this stage, Ruth told herself, they had the name and address of Anne's parents which was more important, and she went off to tell Matt.

He phoned them at once, two bewildered people who had only just discovered that their daughter was not, as they had thought, happily esconced in a friend's house in Scotland. They had sat all day phoning around different friends and acquaintances, reluctant at this early stage to contact the police.

Matt's phone call had been an answer to a fervent prayer and though they had only been back from Greece less than a day they made plans to fly out to Jersey at once.

When Ruth saw the travel-weary, ashen-faced, rather dowdy looking middle-aged couple at Jersey Airport her previous judgment of them did a right-about turn, and the only feeling she had at that moment was pity. They weren't a bit as she had expected Anne's parents to look; their only physical link with their daughter was that like her they had fine dark eyes. Mrs Marshall was short and on the stocky side, her husband was tall with a stoop, and they were both dressed in shapeless tweeds. Ruth noticed that they held hands, and she found that touching, though perhaps Anne had seen it differently. Perhaps she had seen in that gesture two self-contained people who only needed each other.

All this Ruth chewed over in her mind now as she walked slowly along the path that she had come to know intimately by every twist and turn. It was her free afternoon and she had escaped from the house that seemed to mock her with its emptiness since Anne and her baby had gone.

Matt had taken the Marshalls to the surgery, opened the door to Anne's room and had let them go in on their own. Both he and Ruth were busy with the afternoon patients and didn't see the Marshalls again until they had a break for tea. There were traces of tears in their eyes then, but the look of strain in their faces had lessened. They couldn't find words enough to express their gratitude for what had been done for their daughter. Mrs Marshall said once as if to herself: 'When I think of what might have happened to her if—' She gave a little shiver and her husband took her hand, in comfort.

There were plans to make as to where they could stay. Matt offered them a room in St Swithin House but they wouldn't hear of that.

'We've imposed on you enough already,' said Mr Marshall, looking up with a sad smile from under shaggy brows. 'Perhaps you could recommend a hotel near at hand?'

'I hear that the Mirabelle is very good and that's the nearest,' answered Matt without hesitation. He looked at Ruth; there was no rancour or irony in his voice. He was just stating a fact.

The following afternoon Mrs Marshall walked with Ruth in the garden, she seemed to want to unburden herself to someone and she felt closer to Ruth than anyone else at hand. She had a low pleasant voice, and she spoke hesitantly at first as if choosing her words carefully.

'We didn't deserve Florence—no Anne, as I must call her now—' She broke off with a quiet smile. 'She insists on that, she never did like the name Florence. We named her after the city, you know—where we had spent our honeymoon, and even that was a snub in a way, though we didn't intend it as such, but we commemorated in our child the memory of a wonderful experience that had happened twenty years before she was born. It was our first visit to Florence; we are both art historians, and the beauty of the architecture and the paintings of the Renaissance went to our heads like wine. That is our career—chasing the world after art treasures, failing to realise that the greatest gift of beauty ever given to us was our own daughter. We didn't deserve her; we could, in our ignorance, have destroyed that rare spirit of serenity she possesses. It wasn't that we didn't love her—I think in our stupid bumbling way we were frightened of her, as if she were some exquisite piece of statuary to be left on the shelf and admired rather than handled. It was a relief to us that she never made demands on us. She was an extraordinary child, she rarely cried and she had infinite patience. I can't remember her ever whining or grizzling. She accepted whatever happened to her with complete fortitude and never complained. No wonder we took advantage of her.' Adèle Marshall gave a listless sigh. 'We just counted ourselves lucky that we had a model child who never expected anything from us. We used to boast to our friends that having a child had made no difference to our lives whatsoever, that we could still carry on our careers without hindrance. What fools we were—we didn't ask ourselves what our neglect had made to the quality of Anne's life.

'Then we arrived back from Greece and discovered that Anne was missing, that's when we came face to face with reality. You know what they say about drowning people seeing the whole of their lives flashing before their eyes? That's what happened to Victor and me. We saw it so clearly—the mistakes, the lost opportunities—we knew that if we lost Anne nothing on this earth could make it up to us.'

Adèle paused and carefully wiped her eyes. She was pale but more composed when she spoke again. 'Well, we *have* been given the chance to make amends. Another little Anne has been sent to us and this time, please God, we'll take more care of her. We have learnt our lesson, we are humble and proud that we've been given this second opportunity.'

Ruth didn't answer immediately, wondering if the Marshalls would go too far in the opposite direction—become too possessive and smother the child with too much love. But seeing Mrs Marshall so contrite, she didn't think this was probable. As she said, she had learnt her lesson—and so, in a different way, had Anne.

'Have you decided on a name for the baby?' Ruth asked as they retraced their steps towards the house.

The older woman gave a wistful laugh. 'Would you believe, all we can agree on is Anne. I think because everybody has been calling the baby Little Anne she seems to have grown into the name. I'm glad, I like the old-fashioned names.'

Adèle was silent for a while, then she said, 'Did Anne tell you that when she was really down on her luck and had no money left to buy food, she thought she'd try to sell her hair? She got the idea from one of her grandmother's books she found in the house, *Little Women*. Thank God nothing came of it; she got as far as the hairdressing salon and then lost her nerve—not that I think she would have succeeded. Who buys hair these days!'

'How did she manage for food then?' cried Ruth in distress, remembering the way Anne had eaten the biscuits as if starving.

'She sold something more practical; her great-grandfather's stamp-album, and the rogue in the junk shop gave her one pound-fifty for it. Some of the stamps alone are worth much more than that each! Victor has gone off this afternoon to get it back, I don't think he'll have any problem. Anne spent the money on bread, and that's all she had to live on until the day she went into labour. It's a miracle to me that the baby is so healthy. Anne says she'll never forget the taste of those eggs you served her after Little Anne was born. I'll never forget to the day I die the debt I owe you—' Adèle's voice broke. 'You've all been so good—so very good, we can never repay you.'

She couldn't go on, she was on the verge of tears.

Ruth changed the subject to the one that had been
on her mind for days. 'Did she tell you who the
father is?'

'No, the barrier comes down whenever I ask her.
But I can guess and I hope I'm right because I can
see a chance of them coming together eventually,
perhaps when we've been able to persuade Anne
that he has nothing to fear from the law. He's the
son of my oldest friend, and in his final year at
university. This friend was a widow and she and her
son spent Christmas with us. The young ones were
thrown together, we oldies encouraged it—we wanted
to talk about old times, listen to music, play cards.
They got on very well together and we could see
Anne had a crush on the young man. She came out
of her shell that holiday and surprised us all, she
was so different—so vital. That's why I can never
condemn her for what happened. Jonathan gave her
what we had denied her most—time and trouble.
Anyway, he returned to college and Anne went back
to school, and I don't know whether they were ever
in contact again. I thought she seemed rather
subdued when she came home for half-term, but
then as she's naturally quiet I didn't attach any
importance to it. Then Victor's mother died and we
were going backwards and forwards to Jersey settling
up her affairs and Christmas seemed way back in
the past. My friend remarried and went off to
Canada with her new husband and I lost touch with
Jonathan. If he is the father,' Adèle went on
thoughtfully, 'and really wants to marry Anne and
if Anne wants to marry him, we won't stand in her
way, but speaking as someone who has had experience of students' marriages, I think it would be wiser
if she waits until she has got her own degree. Still,
I'm not going to influence her one way or the

other—I've made a pretty poor mother up to now, so I'm really in no position to give advice. The first thing is to get Anne really well and to build up her health again, and I think in time when I have obtained her full confidence we'll be able to discuss her future quite openly.'

Anne was well enough to face the journey back to her parents' home by the following Saturday. She had been at St Swithin House exactly a week, and a week of Ruth's nursing, Mrs Miller's care and Pam's cooking had fleshed out her stick-like arms and given a rose-coloured tint to her olive skin just above the high cheekbones. They were all rather tearful to see her go, especially Mrs Miller who cried openly. Even little Robbie was affected. He had struck up quite a friendship with Anne. She never questioned the reason for his speechlessness and it didn't appear to worry her. The small boy and the teenage girl seemed to be able to communicate without words. Anne had a gift for music and could make the recorder sing like a bird, and under her tuition Robbie soon learnt to play a few simple tunes himself.

Only that morning, five days after they had left Jersey, presents had arrived from the Marshalls for everyone at St Swithin House. Cashmere scarves for Pam and Stephanie—'What have I done to deserve this!' exclaimed Stephanie. 'I only took Anne's temperature on one occasion.' A silk blouse for Mrs Miller, a watch for Matt, and in a separate parcel addressed to Ruth, a beautiful satin and lace night-gown. There was an enclosed note with it. 'Exchange is no robbery. I made use of two of yours. Anne.'

'It's far too gorgeous to wear in bed—it's more like an evening gown,' Ruth said, holding it up for them all to admire.

'I agree with you, it is too good for everyday wear, you must put it away in your bottom drawer. You'll delight your bridegroom in it,' said Mrs Miller in all seriousness.

'She'll delight him a lot more out of it,' said Pam *sotto voce*. Ruth heard her and so did Matt. Ruth fled with scarlet cheeks from the enigmatic look he threw her.

Matt had been in an odd mood since the Marshalls had left, though always friendly. The old dour melancholy that had so intimidated Ruth during her first days in Jersey had gone, and in its place was a friendliness so detached and constrained that it left her on edge. It was as if Matt was schooling himself to be nice to her when his natural instincts were quite the reverse. She suspected he was bored with her. Her month was nearly up and nothing had been said about renewing her contract, though as far as she knew no arrangements had been made to replace her. Mrs Sudbury wouldn't be well enough to come back to work for several weeks. Ruth had told Stephanie about the job awaiting her at St Catherine's and it must have got back to Matt, but he didn't mention it. The last time they had a conversation together that didn't hinge on work was when the results of her blood count had come through. Dr Goodson had given her a clean bill of health.

'That news must be a relief to you,' Matt had said, giving her a long steady look out of hazel eyes that successfully masked his feelings.

'That's no thanks to myself. I've been forgetting to take my iron tablets regularly. It's Jersey—it's the wonderful air here, the feeling of relaxation.'

Matt had laughed at that, throwing his head back and giving a loud untuneful bellow. It was the first time Ruth had heard him laugh and to her it sounded false—there seemed an edge of desperation to it.

'That's rich,' he glinted at her in his old sardonic manner. 'You've only been with us two weeks and in that time you've set us all on our heads and righted us again. You've even produced a pregnancy out of the air and then stage-managed the end result. You call that relaxation!'

She went pink. 'I—I'm sorry I've caused so much disruption,' she said ruefully.

His expression changed, his tone softened. 'Not disruption, Ruth—a better word for it would be therapy. You've done us all a power of good.'

She carried that last look he gave her about with her for days. She didn't get the chance to be alone with him again. He had been called to the hospital to help out with a mystery virus that was knocking victims down like nine-pins, giving them symptoms of vertigo and nausea. It only lasted three days, but was very unpleasant while it lasted. Stephanie and Ruth coped with the surgery on their own.

And now Ruth was free for a few hours, glad of this chance to air her thoughts alone, wanting more than anything to indulge in visualising Matt. She could conjure up his image at will—the strong line of his jaw, the deep-set hazel eyes, the heavy dark brows that seemed to take on a life of their own, lifting together or coming together in a frown, though the latter not so frequently as in her early days.

Ruth knew that when she left Jersey she would leave part of her heart behind and the thought of never seeing Matt again was an ache that would never lessen. Without realising it she had walked as far as the cliff where an overhanging ledge of grass and tangled scrub hid the jagged cleft below. She often thought of the dream she had had on her second night in Jersey, seeing Matt standing where she was standing now with such a look of despair on his face. Dreams always mean the opposite, she had been told. It was *she* who was standing in the fatal spot—it was *she* who felt the despair.

'What has happened to my sea-nymph?' asked a playful voice behind her. 'You look more like a lost soul in torment.'

Ruth turned with a gesture of impatience to the man who had stolen up on her unawares. 'I wish you wouldn't do that. I hate people sneaking up behind me.'

Tony Graver grinned. 'I couldn't resist it—you were miles away. What were you thinking about?'

'Nothing,' she said quickly—too quickly. 'Well, as a matter of fact,' she conceded, 'it's this particular spot—it makes me nervous, gives me a feeling of apprehension.' Ruth could barely repress a shiver. 'And I felt like that before I found out that it was here Mrs Owens tried to commit suicide.'

'What do you mean—*tried* to commit suicide!' Tony sneered.

Ruth turned on him angrily. 'Once before you hinted that Matt—Dr Owens—had got rid of his wife in some mysterious way. Are you trying to suggest that she didn't commit suicide? That *someone* pushed her over the cliff?'

'No need to get hysterical.' Tony looked nervously around but there was no one to hear their altercation. Ruth's reaction had shaken him. What he had said had been out of pure malice because he had a few scores to settle with Matt Owens. Now he realised he had gone too far.

'I'm not making any accusations,' he said grudgingly. 'I'm only saying that Colette disappeared in very fishy circumstances. I know all about her suicide attempt, it was common knowledge at the time, but just supposing she had another go later and this time succeeded. The Owens wouldn't have cared for that bit of scandal to be bruited around, would they? Much better to let it be thought that Mrs Owens had died naturally in some far-off nursing home.'

Hot words of rebuttal died on Ruth's lips. She recalled that Sheila Sudbury had said nobody had actually *seen* Colette leave St Swithin—everybody had accepted Matt's words that she had died in London. And why shouldn't they? Matt was a man of integrity.

Ruth drew a tongue over dry lips and regarded Tony with challenging eyes. 'You're in no position to accuse anybody of anything,' she said. 'You knew she had a drink problem yet you encouraged her to go to the Mirabelle. It was the drink that nearly drove her to suicide.'

Tony winced, Ruth's words had caught him on the raw. He answered fiercely, 'I can well imagine who started that filthy lie. Let me tell you, Colette needed no encouragement to come to the Mirabelle —it was her refuge. My worry was to keep her out when the drink got the better of her. I couldn't stand by and watch her destroy herself like that.' He added menacingly, 'If Matt Owens has any accusations to make he should have the guts to make them to my face, not send an emissary. The man's despicable!'

'He isn't!' Ruth cried, angry tears springing to her eyes. 'He isn't despicable and he hasn't accused you of anything. I-It's something someone else said that made me jump to that conclusion. Matt has never mentioned your name in connection with his wife—not once!'

Tony stared at the quivering girl in wonder, and

all the fight went out of him. 'You're in love with the fellow, aren't you?'

Ruth didn't deny it, there was no point. Tony gave her a pitying smile.

'You poor kid, I had no idea it had got as far as that.' He shrugged. 'All right, I'll take back what I said; he's not despicable, but he's no angel either. He's a cold-hearted fish and nobody will ever convince me that he wasn't to blame for Colette's death.'

'You're jealous of him,' said Ruth with a sudden insight. 'You loved her!'

Tony made no denial either. He gave another shrug and this time his mouth twisted in a bitter grimace. 'I could have made Colette happy,' he said dejectedly. 'I could make her laugh—that's more than that Owens fellow ever managed. I could even have made her forget Jacques Bonet, her first husband. Matt Owens didn't have much success there either.'

Tony tried to summon up his old air of urbanity but without much success. He held out his hand. 'I doubt whether our paths will cross again,' he said. 'I've put in for a transfer to another Hackett hotel. I never intended to stay here longer than was necessary to get the Mirabelle off the ground so my transfer is long overdue. I'm sorry if I've upset you, Ruth—' he broke off, then added wryly, 'I think you and I could have had something going for us given the time—but there, we're both birds of passage, we didn't get the chance.'

Ruth wished he hadn't said that—the very words Matt had uttered on her first day at St Swithin bringing back bitter-sweet longings that could never be fulfilled. She watched Tony walk away without really noticing him, engrossed in mulling over what he had said.

Could Colette have made a second, successful attempt at taking her life, and could Matt have covered it up, putting out that story about her dying in a London nursing home? Oh yes, he was quite capable of doing that, but not for the reason Tony supposed—not because of the DeBrice pride. For another reason altogether—little Robbie. Ruth knew there was no sacrifice Matt wouldn't make, no lie he wouldn't tell, to spare his son further suffering.

All that evening Ruth wrestled with wild ideas that floated in and out of her mind. If only, before she went back to Norfolk, some miracle would happen and little Robbie recover his powers of speech. In her present state of mind she felt that would be the answer to all the problems besieging St Swithin House. If Robbie was a normal boy again his father might feel free to speak of the secret that haunted him. She gave her imagination free rein, weaving schemes that might lay the scene for such a miracle to happen.

For instance, she told herself later as she lay sleepless, watching the moon sailing the night sky, Robbie had shown his terror of the cliff. It was there that he had received the shock that had made him mute, so couldn't another shock in the same place perhaps jolt him back into speaking once again?

What kind of shock? Ruth asked herself—but she already knew the answer. If Robbie were to witness another incident similar to his mother's suicide, would that do the trick? Or would it be cruel to play such a trick on such a susceptible child? Ruth shuddered as she realised what she was asking of herself—to pretend to fall over the cliff so that Robbie would be frightened enough to scream for help. And suppose she did manage to make it look like a real fall, and Robbie didn't scream—or even worse, collapsed from terror. How could she face Matt then? How to explain!

Ruth tossed and turned for most of the night and woke up the next morning with a raging head. Stephanie didn't notice her silence at breakfast, she herself seemed to have something on her mind. Something very pleasurable going by the look of deep happiness that sparkled occasionally in her blue eyes. During the past few days Ruth had come across Stephanie and Matt several times talking quietly together as if discussing something private. Ruth didn't have to search very far for a reason. She told herself she was mad to want to stay and witness their growing attachment, but given the chance she would have stayed on—her heart overruled her judgement.

Her plane was leaving Sunday afternoon. On Saturday morning she would make that desperate attempt to break Robbie's silence. If it came off it would be her farewell gift to Matt. If it didn't work—well, at least she had tried.

Fate, in the shape of a shaggy, unruly, overgrown puppy, sent the miracle Ruth had prayed for. She had persuaded Robbie to come for a walk with her, and he had agreed happily enough, but the recorder had to come along too.

They were halfway to the fatal spot where Ruth had decided to stage her drama when a large young dog appeared from nowhere and dropped a ball at Robbie's feet. Robbie obliged, stooped to pick it up and the dog, all excitement, knocked the recorder out of his hand. What came next happened in the blink of an eyelid. The dog forgot all about the ball, snatched up the recorder instead and bounded away with it.

Ruth, seeing the horror that welled into Robbie's face, immediately gave chase. Gone were all thoughts of a pretence of an accident involving the cliffs—more urgent was the necessity of retrieving the simple instrument that was so precious to the small boy.

Ruth caught up with the dog near the cliff top and then began the battle for the possession of the recorder, the dog thinking it a game and growling with delight as she tried to take it away from him. Then a sudden whistle in the distance froze him into immobility. He cocked an ear, dropped his hold and galloped away. Ruth, still pulling, lost her balance and fell, and began to roll towards the edge of the cliff.

She grabbed frantically at some scrub as she slithered past, but it came away in her hand. Then fortunately she got a grip on a tougher, thicker branch and was able to haul herself to safety.

Ruth crouched on the grass panting, realising how near she had been to plunging to her death. She realised too what a stupid fool she had been to think of staging a similar 'accident', vowing that never again would she allow her imagination to trick her into such foolhardiness. Then above the sound of the seagulls' keening she thought she could hear a long-drawn, unnatural wail. Another sea-bird perhaps, one she didn't recognise.

Wearily she picked up the recorder and began the trek back to Robbie. He was where she had left him—he hadn't moved, but his mouth was open and he was *screaming*.

Ruth ran to him and clasped him in her arms. He couldn't stop screaming, he was in a state of hysteria.

She knew she should slap him or shake him to bring him out of it but she couldn't bring herself to do either. He was making such a thin pitiful attempt at a scream—but he was making sound! Ruth began to cry, first with gratefulness that quite inadvertently a miracle had happened, then with reaction at her near-escape, and finally from all the pent-up emotions of the past few weeks.

It was a good hard bout of sobbing and it acted on Robbie like a slap. He stopped screaming and said: 'Ruth—Ruth, don't cry.' Then he started to cry himself.

It was an emotional pair that Matt came upon very shortly afterwards. Pam had told him that Ruth and Robbie had gone for a walk and he decided to join them. There was a lot he wanted to talk over with Ruth, and lately he hadn't had much opportunity to get her on her own.

He saw them a little way ahead, Ruth sitting on the grass with Robbie on her lap. They were both sitting very still but something about their attitudes started his heart hammering. He hurried his stride.

'What's up—what's happened?' he asked abruptly as he came up to them. 'Why are you sitting like this? Why are you so pale?' He stared at Ruth.

The strength had come back to her legs now, the shaking had stopped. She got to her feet and helped Robbie to his. 'Robbie,' she said gently. 'Say something to Daddy.'

'I speaked,' said Robbie.

Ruth heard Matt's sharp intake of breath, she saw the blood drain from his face and the fire of hope that suddenly sparked in his eyes. She saw him go down on his knees and take his son into his arms, and she walked quickly away. This was their hour.

She found refuge in the room where she had waited that first day at St Swithin House. It was rarely used and she could sit there on her own, quietly fighting to regain her composure until it was time to face the others.

And it was here Matt came to her, after searching for her without success elsewhere. He sat on the sofa beside her and took her hand tenderly in his. His face was haggard, and white with fatigue, and his eyes looked hot with unshed tears, but there was a look of peace in his expression that has been missing before.

'Robbie is sleeping. His voice is a bit rusty, but it will improve. He managed to tell me what happened. My God, Ruth, when I think what might have happened to you—' Matt broke off, unable to finish the sentence.

His words filled Ruth with a sudden hope which faded when she realised he might be in the grip of an emotion built on gratitude and nothing more. 'You see, it *was* another shock that made it possible for Robbie to speak again,' she reminded him. 'He thought he had lost his recorder.'

Matt dismissed this with a faint shake of his head. 'No, it was you he thought he'd lost. He saw you falling and closed his eyes—then he screamed.' Matt gave her a weak smile. 'But I grant you that recorder may have had something to do with his voice coming back. He has been piping away on it continuously these past few weeks, and that could have lubricated his larynx and eased up his tightened muscles. I'll take him to see an ENT specialist next week and have some tests made—perhaps speech therapy will help too. But I mustn't rush things, I must give him time to recover naturally.'

'I think I ought to tell you . . .' Ruth hesitated,

not knowing how to phrase her words without sounding too dramatic. 'That fall I had—that was unintentional, but I had planned to fake one—to fall over the cliff, I mean, in order to shock Robbie into speaking again.' Now that she had started she had to go on, had to bring all her doubts and fears into the open. 'It was something Tony Graver said about—about your wife. I thought perhaps she had made a second attempt at suicide and had succeeded. I thought if—if perhaps I could get Robbie to speak again it would be such a comfort to you that it would make up to you all that you had been through—give you back your peace of mind.' Her voice broke, then faded away. She had said more than she intended, aware that Matt had stiffened and was sitting like a graven image. In the silence that followed Ruth could hear her heart beating like a time bomb inside her head.

Then Matt turned her to face him and gave her a long hard look. 'Does my peace of mind matter so much to you?' he asked quietly.

'Yes.' Just that one word, but it told Matt all he wanted to know.

He took her into his arms and stared searchingly into her eyes. 'Does that mean you love me?'

'Yes—yes!' She had no pride now, no scruples —only submission. She heard him give a quiet moan, then he crushed his lips to hers in a passion that made her senses leap, but she knew it was a passion backed by a cherishing and caring love.

He drew her to her feet. 'Come along,' he said, reverting to his old masterly manner. 'What I have to say to you isn't going to be told in this gloomy old room. Let's go out to the garden, to your favourite walk under the pines.'

Patches of blue were beginning to show between

the clouds, summer still had a little to offer. And walking arm in arm, feeling Matt's warmth and strength engulfing her, Ruth heard the full and tragic story of Colette.

He first knew Colette before she married Jacques Bonet. They mixed in the same circles and he was infatuated with her then. He described her as delicate and fey like a piece of Dresden china. Then Bonet came on the scene—literally sailed into her life from St Malo in his beautiful gleaming white yacht the *Bonne Nuit*.

'I don't know what possessed Bonet to marry Colette,' Matt exclaimed resignedly. 'He could so easily have had her for his mistress—she was besotted with him, and they were so wrong for each other. He, the worldly young playboy, wealthy, sought after, spoilt; and she—' Matt gave a despairing shrug. 'Just that fragile beauty, nothing else. Of course she couldn't hold him and that's when the drinking started. First to give her the courage to mix with his friends, then because she discovered she couldn't face the day without it.'

The marriage was dissolved after two years. Jacques Bonet brought his wife back to St Helier and left her, (dumped her, said her friends). He made her a good allowance, considered he had done all that was required of him and faded out of her life, leaving somebody else to pick up the pieces.

'I was arrogant enough to think I could make her happy, even to forget her unhappy experience. I thought I could cure her of her drinking problem, so I married her and brought her to St Swithin.' Matt's bitterness was directed at himself. He blamed nobody but himself that this marriage in turn was a failure.

'She was never going to get over Jacques Bonet,'

Matt said after one of his poignant silences. 'She didn't want to get over him. She used to drive to St Helier—this was before her licence was taken away from her—and hang about the harbour for hours, longing and hoping for the *Bonne Nuit* to sail into port. I thought if she had a child it would give her something else to think about, that a child might bring us closer together. She didn't want to have a child, she begged me not to give her one, but again I was too arrogant to take notice—I wouldn't accept that there are some women not cut out for mother-hood.'

Colette had a difficult confinement that left her in a state of depression, and then the drinking started again, this time worse. Matt banned all drink from the house, but by this time the Mirabelle had been built and he couldn't keep her locked up. She had money of her own too, Bonet's money. But now Matt realised there was a change in her drinking pattern. She wasn't drinking to forget her first husband, she was drinking to give herself the courage to face up to her second.

'She didn't hate me exactly,' said Matt drearily. 'And she didn't fear me either, though at times she seemed frightened of me—or rather what I might do to her. Her feeling for me was more like distaste, as if she couldn't bear me near her. She had to drink to give herself the strength to face me across the dining-table, God damn it!'

Ruth ached for him. The despair in his voice was like a wound in her heart, and she could do nothing but tighten her grip on his arm in sympathy. But he understood what she was trying to convey to him, and appreciated it.

'Dear sweet little Ruth. You understand so perfectly, I don't have to spell it out for you word by word. Well, I've nearly finished with poor Colette, then we'll let her lie in peace.'

Matt was now spending his time between London and Jersey. He thought the kindest thing for Colette was to keep away from her as much as possible, but it was an unsatisfactory arrangement and in the meantime Robbie was being neglected. The alternative was to get Colette away from Jersey, away from old memories, perhaps they could try a new beginning in London? But when he suggested this to her she started at once on a frenzied drinking bout. It was in the aftermath of that that she made her abortive suicide attempt.

'After that it was one disaster after another,' said Matt in a saddened voice. 'Little Robbie went mute and Colette sank into an alcoholic coma. Robbie was ill, I didn't want him to sense anything was wrong in case it impeded his recovery. I took Colette away by car on the cross-channel ferry to Southampton. I knew of a private clinic in London that specialised in the treatment of alcoholics, but I was too late by several years. Colette slipped away one night about six weeks later.'

They had come out of the shelter of the woods on to the greensward. The only person in sight was a man some distance away throwing a ball for a dog to retrieve—perhaps the very dog who had worked their miracle.

The sun shone mistily through thin cloud, there was hardly a breath of wind. It was a day of tranquillity and peace, even the sea hardly moved.

Ruth felt a surge of renewed love for this inspired man beside her. He had opened his heart to her, revealed secrets that he had kept locked away for years, and that had left him empty of emotion but free of the old haunting melancholy. She knew he loved her, she could feel it in his touch and see it in his eyes every time he looked at her. She could never be jealous of poor unhappy Colette, but she did wonder about Stephanie and mentioned her name nervously.

Matt gave a short incredulous laugh. 'You thought I loved Stephanie! Oh darling Ruth, I do—but not the way I love you. Just as well really, I wouldn't stand an earthly against a certain white-haired general practitioner whose ship should dock in less than forty-eight hours.'

Sudden understanding widened her eyes, made her gape. 'You don't mean . . .?'

'My father, yes. Surprised?' This time Matt's laugh was of sheer delight. Laughter lines wiped out the old marks of suffering, and made him look years younger. Laughter can change a person's whole demeanour, and Matt hadn't laughed like that in years.

'Yes, I am surprised,' Ruth retorted, thinking of the hours of unnecessary heartache the misunderstanding had caused her. 'I heard Stephanie on the phone to you one evening—at least, I thought it was you.'

'She told me about that phone call. Dad phoned her from Tobago of all places, to tell her he had found the ideal honeymoon spot. They had kept their engagement secret because of Mrs Miller, but she had guessed.'

'Why Mrs Miller?' interrupted Ruth, astounded. She couldn't think of a less likely rival.

'Because they didn't want her to give in her notice. She has made herself invaluable in spite of her touchiness, and they knew they could never get another housekeeper as good. Stephanie didn't want to give up medicine so she needed someone to run the house, but unfortunately Mrs Miller looked upon Stephanie as a threat rather than an ally. Or rather she did.'

So much was plain to Ruth now. The confidences Stephanie and Matt shared—the sour looks from Mrs Miller.

'How do you mean—did?' she asked.

'Haven't you noticed the change that has come over Mrs Miller lately? She's mellowed—we all have. It's your influence, Ruth. You brought something fresh and vital into this tired old household. You brought fresh hope and a chance for new beginnings. You came to this island to be cured, but it's you who have worked a cure on us instead. Do you know what it is?'

'No,' she said shyly, overcome by the demanding look that flared suddenly into his eyes.

'The ultimate cure, my darling, is—love.'

There was so much more to plan—their futures, Robbie's future; a future that included both London and Jersey, St Jude's and St Catherine's. But that could wait—Matt couldn't. Ruth went willingly into his arms.

Doctor Nurse Romances

A TALE OF ILLICIT LOVE

'Defy the Eagle' is a stirring romance set in
Roman Britain at the time of Boadicea's rebellion.
Caddaric is an Iceni warrior loyal to his Queen. The lovely
Jilana is a daughter of Rome and his sworn enemy.
Will their passion survive the hatred of war,
or is the cost too great?
A powerful new novel from Lynn Bartlett.

W⬤RLDWIDE

Price: £3.50   Available: August 1987

Available from Boots, Martins, John Menzies, W.H. Smith,
Woolworths and other paperback stockists.